"SO YOU'RE GOING TO RUN, THROW IT ALL AWAY, BECAUSE YOU HAVEN'T THE GUTS TO GROW UP."

Sam glared at him. "What do you mean, throw it all away?"

Morgan's eyes were as cold as his voice. "I mean there'll be no polite little visits every now and then, so you don't lose the money. I'll divorce you, Samantha, and you can live off your stepmother until you find a man who'll marry you under your conditions. Or you might fall in love, if you're capable, and the physical side of it won't be so abhorrent to you."

"You really are a beast," she whispered.

"Maybe so," he said. "But that's beside the point. It's up to you. You can go or stay. But make no mistake, if you stay, what happened last night will happen again regularly. If you go now, it will be final. So make up your mind. What's it going to be, go or stay?"

MORGAN WADE'S WOMAN

Amii Lorin

A CANDLELIGHT ECSTASY CLASSIC ROMANCE

Published by
Dell Publishing Co., Inc.
1 Dag Hammarskjold Plaza
New York, New York 10017

A Candlelight Ecstasy Classic Romance

Candlelight Ecstasy Romance®, 1,203,540, is a registered trademark of
Dell Publishing Co., Inc.

ISBN: 0-440-15507-X

Printed in the United States of America

One Previous Edition

July 1987

10 9 8 7 6 5 4 3 2 1

WFH

To Our Readers:

By popular demand we are happy to announce that we will be bringing you two Candlelight Ecstasy Classic Romances every month.

In the upcoming months your favorite authors and their earlier best-selling Candlelight Ecstasy Romances® will be available once again.

As always, we will continue to present the distinctive sensuous love stories that you have come to expect only from Ecstasy and also the very finest work from new authors of contemporary romantic fiction.

Your suggestions and comments are always welcome. Please write to us at the address below.

Sincerely,

The Editors
Candlelight Romances
1 Dag Hammarskjold Plaza
New York, New York 10017

CHAPTER 1

Sam pushed through the doors of the tall building that housed the offices of Baker, Baker, and Simmes, Attorneys-at-law, and stood tapping her foot impatiently on the sidewalk. Where was her driver? She was only vaguely aware of the admiring glances turned her way by men passing, both on foot and motorized. She had only to step onto a public street at any time to receive these glances and, quite often, to her disgust, remarks as well.

That Samantha Denning was a strikingly beautiful woman there was no doubt. She stood five feet eight inches in her slim, stockinged feet. She was very slender, with long perfectly shaped legs and softly rounded curves exactly where they belonged. Her face was a perfect oval, the skin fair, with creamy pink cheeks, and a short, straight nose above full red lips that covered perfectly shaped white teeth. Dark brows arched gracefully over large, deep-green eyes, the lids heavily fringed with long, dark lashes. But what one saw first was her hair. Thick, long, wavy, not quite red, but more the color of highly polished, expensive mahogany. It seemed, when it hung loose, to have a will of its own. Subdued now in a coil around her head, it offset perfectly the severely but expensively cut hunter green suit she wore. With a large leather shoulder bag, snug leather gloves, and high-heeled boots, all black, her somewhat somber look was the only concession she would give to mourning clothes. They were none too effective, however, as a few curly tendrils at her temple and in front of her ears had escaped their pins and danced merrily on her face in the soft spring breeze, defying the impression of the dark suit and black accessories.

Samantha tapped her foot even more impatiently as, glancing at the narrow platinum watch on her slim wrist, she thought, *Damn, where is that man?* Looking up, she saw the long, midnight-blue Cadillac glide to a stop opposite her at the curb. Before she took the few steps required to reach the car, the driver had jumped out of the front seat and was holding the door to the back open for her. As he touched her elbow lightly to help her enter, she said crossly, "Where have you been?"

"Sorry, Miss Sam, but the traffic's pretty heavy," he murmured. She glanced out the window to note the truth of his excuse, realizing she had been so deep in thought while she waited she hadn't even noticed.

"Yes, I see, I'm sorry I snapped, Dave. I'm going home now."

Dave smiled to himself as he pulled the big car into the stream of traffic. It was like her to apologize for snapping at him. She was self-willed, haughty, and imperious most of the time with her family and friends, but rarely ever did she speak sharply with the employees.

Dave had been with the Dennings fifteen years now, he as chauffeur and his wife, Beth, as a cook. They respected Mr. Denning, liked his petite, delicate, second wife, and were fond of her young half-sister Deborah. But they both adored Sam, this rebellious, redheaded firebrand, from the day she had come to the big house on Long Island to stay. Dave smiled again as he drove the car expertly through midtown Manhattan toward home, remembering that day seven years before.

What an uproar the house had been in, Mrs. Denning wanting everything perfect for the first meeting with her stepdaughter. Even Mr. Denning's normal reserve seemed about to crack as he and Dave waited for her plane to land. They had expected a shy seventeen-year-old and what they saw walking toward them was a queen.

She had said lightly and unselfconciously, kissing his cheek, "Hello, father," and then had turned as Mr. Denning said in introduction, "This is our driver, Dave Zimmer."

He had been wearing the usual gray uniform and he chuckled to himself now as he remembered the way her eyes had looked him up and down.

"Not mine, not dressed like that at any rate. I'd as soon drop dead as be seen being driven by a liveried chauffeur."

That said, she'd given him the most beautiful smile he'd ever seen and added, "Please, Mr. Dave, could you not wear your everyday clothes if you have ever to drive me?"

He had been lost from that moment. It had been about the same when they had reached the house. Within ten minutes she had overawed her tiny stepmother and equally small halfsister and enslaved the rest of the employees. She had ruled the roost ever since.

He had heard the story years ago, how the quiet, reserved Charles Denning had gone to England on a business trip and returned four months later with a ravishingly beautiful wife from a wealthy British family. Being a wealthy man himself, he had bought the huge house on Long Island for her. But nothing seemed to content her, not her husband or the house or even the daughter she bore eighteen months after their marriage. She missed her friends at home and refused to make new ones in her husband's homeland, referring to them all as gauche. When Samantha was two, she fled to her family, taking the girl with her. Though Charles Denning had fought for custody of his child, his ex-wife's family was powerful and he had to be satisfied with a few visits during those years.

Immediately on Samantha's mother's death, he had instructed his lawyers to notify the family that Samantha was to come to him. She had been back at school in Switzerland when she received the news and requested he allow her to finish her schooling and go ahead with plans made to do her tour of Europe with an American girl she'd been friends with in school for years. Her father had acquiesced to her request but had sworn that when he finally had her home he would keep her there.

Taking a cigarette from her bag and lighting it, Sam leaned back against the pale-blue plush upholstery, looking completely calm and relaxed. Inside she was fuming. How could he do this? Why? She went over it again in her mind, the meeting she had just come from and what had precipitated it.

They had gathered in the library the afternoon before. Her stepmother, Mary, calm now from the tranquilizer her doctor had given her, her half sister, Deb, still looking pale and a little lost, Deb's fiancé, Bryan Tyson, and Sam. Mr. Baker had asked them to assemble at three for the reading of the will. The reading had gone along smoothly without interruption with Mr. Baker's voice droning on about bequests for the employees; then he went on to the family. He went into great detail about what was to be left to Deb and Bryan after their marriage. Sam was very surprised as she learned of the enormity of her father's estate and was deep in thought when Mr. Baker said her name and proceeded with her father's wishes concerning her.

At first Sam stared at him, stunned, then almost sprang from her chair.

"I will not do it. I'll contest the will."

Mr. Baker coughed slightly. "My father thought you would react this way," he replied, "so he instructed me to ask you if you could see him in his office to discuss this tomorrow morning at ten?"

"I'll be there," she said grimly and left the room, not waiting to hear the rest of the will. She had gone to her bedroom to pace the white fur rug, unseeingly touching furniture and the lovely things she had collected over the years. The beautiful room, all white and gold, failed to give her the soothing feeling it usually did. She had been thoroughly agitated and wondered how she could stand it till the morning.

As Sam snubbed out her cigarette, she went over that meeting of an hour ago. Both young Mr. Baker and old Mr. Baker (he had to be in his eighties, although he looked twenty years younger) had been there. Mr. Baker the elder had come directly to the point.

"Miss Denning, I see no way you can possibly break your father's will."

She had been in the process of lighting a cigarette, and he was watching her hands, beautiful hands with long, slender fingers, the nails gracefully oval-shaped, covered with pink polish. The lighter closed loudly in the quiet room. Sam inhaled deeply before replying.

"I don't see why. The terms are ridiculous."

"Not at all, Miss Denning, and not at all unusual."

Well, they certainly seemed so to her. She heard again in her mind Mr. Baker's voice yesterday as he read the stipulations to her inheritance.

11

1. If she married an American citizen by the day she was twenty-five (just five months away) she would receive the sum of five million dollars, to be controlled by the husband and Mr. Baker, with a generous monthly allowance for her own personal use.
2. If in five years time the marriage was still intact; the control of the money would revert to herself and her husband jointly.
3. If the marriage was dissolved within said five-year period, the money would revert back to her father's estate, leaving her with a much smaller monthly allowance.
4. If she chose not to marry within the stipulated time, she was to have a small monthly allowance and a home with her stepmother until such time as she did marry or died.

"I'll forfeit," Sam had declared. "I still have my inheritance from my mother." She knew that amounted to approximately two hundred thousand American dollars.

"I'm afraid not, Miss Denning," Mr. Baker murmured. "You see, before your mother died, she changed her will, leaving your father in complete control of your inheritance, and that money is included with your father's."

Sam sat staring at him, speechless. He then went on to explain why he thought she would be unable to break the will, as her father had certainly been in a sound mind when it was drawn up, also his reasons for so stipulating. Oh, Sam knew his reasons. First, he had thought her too headstrong and concluded she needed the firm hand of a husband to control her. Second, he wanted her to make her home permanently in the States, thus the stipulation she must marry an American citizen. The fact that he had

12

set her twenty-fifth birthday as a time limit probably meant he thought the sooner she was safely married the better.

Mr. Baker told Sam that her father had changed the age limit three times in as many years and had given instructions to have it changed again one month before Sam's birthday. His death negated those instructions.

Sam had left the lawyers' office with her mind in turmoil. Now she was almost home and still had not sorted out her thoughts very well. The amount of the inheritance alone staggered her. Five million dollars! Notwithstanding the strings attached, it was an enormous amount of money. Perhaps she should have expected it, for Deb's share was an equal amount. Yet she would not have been hurt or felt left out if she'd have received much less. She had spent a total of nine of her twenty-four years with her father, Deb had been his from birth.

The Cadillac turned in and along the curved driveway slowly, and Sam looked up at the house. It was a beautiful house, an anachronism really, and the cost of maintaining it was staggering. Yet her father would not give it up. He had loved it, and had considered the money well spent.

Sam entered the house and went directly to the small sitting room in search of her stepmother, thinking how unusually quiet the house had seemed since her father's death. She found both Mary and Deb there, sitting close together, talking quietly. Sam sat down in a chair near them, lit a cigarette, dropped her bag and gloves onto the floor beside her, and said, "It seems it would be useless for me to contest the will." Her voice was low and her eyes had an almost lost look.

"Oh, my dear," her stepmother murmured, reaching her small hand out to her. "Please believe I knew nothing of these conditions in your father's will. If I had, I would have tried to dissuade him. They are quite impossible."

"I know, but I don't think it would have helped anyway. He was determined, in his own mind, to tie me down and keep me here." Then, in a stronger voice laced through with anguish, she added, "Didn't he know how much I'd come to love him and this country?" Her voice dropped to a whisper. "Didn't he know?"

Mary and Deb looked at each other helplessly a moment. They had never seen Sam like this. They had seen her angry often, she and her father had gone into battle regularly and they suspected both thoroughly enjoyed it. They had seen her cool and disdainful. But never had they seen this hurt, vulnerable look.

"Samantha," Mary said softly, "you needn't feel you must fulfill these conditions. I'd be happy to supplement your allowance with some of my own."

Sam's voice caught slightly as she replied, "Thank you," and picking up her bag and gloves stood up and said as she walked quickly to the door, "I'll be in my room if you want me, Mother."

Mary called, "Sam," but Sam was already across the hall and on the stairs. Mary turned to Deb with tears in her eyes. "Go to her."

Deb followed Sam up the stairs and into the bedroom. Standing uncertainly inside the door she asked, "Would you like some company?"

Sam smiled at her gently. "Of course, Poppet, sit down, we can talk while I change." Deb sat on the bed and watched as Sam pulled her boots off, slipped off her skirt and jacket, walked across the room to the closet that completely filled one wall, and hung her clothes away neatly.

Deb's eyes went over her half-sister admiringly as she

14

stood there in nothing but panty hose and bra. *What a beautiful thing she is,* Deb thought, and wished again, as she had many times before, that she had met Sam's mother. Deb did not envy Sam anything, except, perhaps at times, her height. Like most petite people she sometimes longed to be tall. But as far as looks went, Deb was honest enough with herself to admit she was not lacking in that department. With her dark hair and very fair skin, she was a lovely woman. Deb also realized that the love she had for this tall sister who had come into her life when she was just thirteen bordered on hero worship.

Pulling the pins out of her hair, Sam walked to the white and gold dressing table, sat down, and picking up her hair brush, began brushing her hair in long slow strokes. Set free, her rich auburn hair hung in deep waves halfway down her back. Deb watched her for a short time, her eyes dark with compassion. "What are you going to do, Sam? Do you know?"

Sam's eyes lifted and met Deb's in the mirror. "I really haven't a clue, Poppet. It's quite a bind."

Deb knew how deeply upset Sam was, for the British accent was heavy. Generally there was just a tinge of it in Sam's speech, becoming thick only when she was very angry or upset.

Pensively Sam added, "My first thought was to find a job, but then, what sort of work could I do?" She paused before adding, "You realize, love, I've been extensively and expensively educated, all of which prepared me to do nothing of use. I can ride, swim, play tennis, and golf with the best, I'm also a fair decoration in any room or gathering. None of these things will earn me a dime." She sighed. "Oh, I suppose I could apply for a post as a salesclerk, but who is going to hire the daughter of Charles Denning once they know?"

15

Deb didn't answer, understanding Sam was sorting it out for herself as well as explaining her options.

"That leaves marriage within five months," Sam went on, "or depending on your mother. The allowance father stipulated in the case I fail to marry in five months' time is less than I've been receiving since the day I first came to this house to live."

"And your mother's inheritance—" Deb began.

"Is tied up with Father's," Sam finished.

"Is there no one you could marry?"

"Oh, there are quite a few I could marry." Sam waved her arms airily. "I must have had at least five proposals of marriage within the last two years, but you see, Poppet, I have no wish to marry any of those men. The idea of spending five days, let alone five years, with any one of them gives me the horrors."

Sam laughed lightly as she walked to the closet and withdrew a white terry robe. "I'm going to take a long hot bath before lunch, maybe that will relax me some. Will you ask Mother to hold lunch a few minutes?"

"Of course," Deb smiled to herself as she left the room. Sam had stopped calling her stepmother Mary and began calling her Mother after their father's death of a heart attack just a week before. The suddenness of his death had shattered his wife and Sam had seemed to take a very protective attitude to both Mary and Deb.

Sam slid her body down into the warm bubbly water and sighed deeply. She wondered now, as she did so often of late, whether she could be an emotional cripple of some sort. She knew she had normal physical urges because she had felt, at times, an almost hurtful, aching need. Yet whenever any of the young men she knew, and there were many, tried to make love to her, she froze. She could respond only lightly to a good-night kiss, and it worried her a little. What she had told Deb was true—the idea of marriage to any of them horrified her. She really didn't know what to do.

Sam woke the next morning to spring sunshine streaming in her windows and a letter postmarked Nevada on her bedside table. "Babs," she said softly, pushing herself into a sitting position as she slit the envelope open. She hadn't heard from her best friend for two months, when Babs had called to tell her her second son had arrived. Sam scanned the pages quickly. Babs began with sincere condolences for all of them, then went on to rhapsodize on the virtues of her youngest. She then came to the most important part of her letter:

> We are having the christening next week and, darling, both Ben and I so want you to be Mark's godmother. You could, of course, stand by proxy, but it would probably do you good to get away for a while at this time, and I do long to see you. Please say you will come. Give my love to the family.
>
> Babs

Sam let the hand holding the letter drop into her lap and mused on it. Should she go? The urge to run had been on her since she'd left the Messrs. Bakers' office. Here was a place to run to. Here was someone to run to. She'd not fallen asleep till very late the night before worrying over what she should do and had reached no decisions. Perhaps talking it over with Babs would help. She had a way of putting things into their proper order of importance. Laughing all the while, Sam thought now, shaking her head and smiling. Sam then sat up straight, swung her long legs off the side of the bed, and picked up the receiver of the white phone that sat on the gilded white and gold table next to her bed. She called her travel agent and made plane reservations for the following Wednesday, then sent a wire to Babs informing her of her arrival day and time.

The big jet was airborne and the seat belt sign blinked out. Sam unfastened her seat belt, moved her seat back, closed her eyes, and relaxed. She felt good and looked it. She hadn't missed the admiring glances sent her way, both in the waiting room, and as she boarded the plane. She was wearing a white crepe long-sleeved blouse with a matching tie at her throat and a soft wool pants suit in a deep shade of pink that set off her almost red hair to perfection. She carried no purse but instead had slung over one shoulder a rather large flight bag in a creamy beige color and wore soft leather high-heeled boots to match.

When she had packed her suitcases she hadn't been quite sure what to take with her. The weather in the East had been unseasonably mild for early March, so she had laid out lightweight clothes. Then on reflection she had put some back into her closet and added a few heavier things. She did not know what the weather was like in the part of Nevada where Babs lived.

Sam smiled slightly to herself with the thought of Babs. Babs of the laughing eyes. Oh, the scrapes Sam had had to extricate her from while they were in school. Babs had an impish streak and had been forever in hot water. Nothing serious, but zany things, usually involving their teachers or later, when they were older, young men. She was bubbly and full of fun and mischief, and to Sam, always cool and composed, fell the task of smoothing the rippled waters. They had become fast friends when they were both twelve years old. The friendship had deepened and

18

matured as the girls grew. They had made the grand tour after leaving school and when Sam had gone to her father in Long Island, Babs had returned to her family in Nevada.

They had been to Europe and Asia together since, and Babs made several shopping trips a year to New York. Then three years ago on one of her trips East, Babs had told Sam she was getting married, almost immediately, to Benjamin Carter, a name Sam had heard often over the years. Babs had assured Sam that she was very much in love, but as she was also very pregnant, couldn't Sam go back to Nevada with her right away and be her maid of honor? Sam went.

Sam had liked Ben Carter on sight. He was a tall, quiet, good-looking young man, and he blatantly adored Babs. The wedding had been a hasty and, as everything involving Babs, hilarious affair, the only off-note being the man whom Ben had wanted as his best man was out of the country and unable to make it back in time for the wedding, much to Ben's disappointment.

Sam had spent just four days in Nevada, and had not seen Babs again until she had made a five-day shopping trip to New York in last August. She had told Sam she was buying a new maternity wardrobe, as she was three months pregnant. They had had a wonderful five days together, making their home base the apartment on the East Side that Sam's father kept for the convenience of the family whenever they had extended stays in the city. She and Babs had torn around shopping all day and had seen a few shows in the evening. Yes, it would be good to see Babs again.

The sign flashed on, Sam fastened her seat belt, then the wheels touched down, and the big plane rolled to a stop. The Las Vegas terminal was, as usual, very busy and Sam stood hesitant a moment. On hearing Babs call her name, she turned to see her and Ben hurrying forward. She smiled as Babs gasped breathlessly, "Oh! We were afraid we were late, we just this minute landed." Ben and Babs lived in the copper regions of the state and kept their own plane for easier mobility.

Babs would always be Babs, and she almost flung herself into Sam's arms, giving her a warm hug. When she stepped back she exclaimed. "It's positively demoralizing for anyone to look as ravishing as you do, Sam . . . how are you?"

"I'm perfectly well, thank you," Sam said, smiling. "You look lovely yourself," she added, her cool eyes going over her friend's slightly full figure. "The extra weight looks good on you."

"Oh, I gained too much carrying Mark." Babs smiled ruefully. "I've still got some to take off."

"You've been saying that for two months," Ben chimed in, but his voice was gentle, and the look he gave his wife caused a odd twist inside Sam.

"Welcome, Sam," he added, putting one arm around her shoulders giving her a light squeeze. "Babs is right, you look terrific."

"Hi, Ben, and thank you, sir," she answered, slipping her arm around his waist to return his hug. "You both look wonderful to me."

Ben laughed. "Now if we can adjourn this meeting of the mutual admiration society, suppose we stop blocking traffic and get out of here."

The women laughed and started moving, Sam asking Babs about the children. That set Babs off, and she went into a discourse about her offspring, talking nonstop, with Sam barely able to get a word in edgewise, while Ben took up Sam's case and led them outside to find a taxi. Finally

Babs came back to earth to say, "We're going to spend the night in Vegas, and fly out to the house in the morning. Okay?" Sam barely had time to smile and nod as Babs rushed on. "I haven't really had a night out since Mark was born and this darling man here has said he is going to buy us a lavish dinner and let me gamble all night if I wish."

"Up to a financial point," Ben said softly, lovingly, as his wife snuggled even closer to him in the back of the cab.

They're so completely, unselfconsciously in love, Sam thought and again felt that twist inside, hating to admit to herself that it was envy. She had always wished only the best for Babs but she could not help thinking if there had been a Ben somewhere for her she would not have this stupid mess she found herself with now. Then she gave a mental shrug, deciding firmly to enjoy her visit with the Carters.

The taxi deposited them at the M.G.M. Grand and Sam looked around curiously as Ben registered for them. It was almost too much to take in at once. The hotel was fantastic, but what caught Sam's attention was the number of people about. It was the middle of the afternoon and everything was crowded.

Babs, watching Sam's face as she looked around, laughed. "You think this is something, wait until tonight." Sam just smiled and still glancing around followed Ben and Babs as they were shown to their rooms. The room was beautifully impersonal, in the manner of good hotels everywhere. Used to staying in the best, Sam nodded her head, glancing around in satisfaction.

They had decided, while still in the cab, to let Sam rest after her flight, and meet for dinner at seven. Babs stated firmly that she intended to nap, as she fully planned to make a night of it.

Sam opened her suitcase, removed the things she'd need for the evening and gave her apple-green lace gown a shake before hanging it up. She then sank into a warm, scented tub. She felt sleepy, she didn't know why, but every plane flight lasting over an hour always left her feeling this way. She was glad Ben and Babs had wanted to stay over. She had never been in Vegas. When she'd come before, she hadn't left the airport, but had gone from one plane to a much smaller one, and flown straight to Babs's parents' home. Sam was curious, as nearly every one of her friends had been to Vegas at least once and had been astonished at finding Sam had not.

Her bath finished, Sam slipped a nightie over her head, called the desk to request a wake-up call at six, and slid between the sheets. She felt deliciously relaxed and wondered idly whom Babs had asked to stand as godfather as she drifted into sleep.

Sam left her room a few minutes before seven, to find Babs and Ben right outside her door. Her eyes went over the two of them appreciatively. Babs was still something to see, even with the added pounds. Small and very fair, with almost white-blond hair and dark-brown brows and lashes on a lovely face with flawless skin, she had a small, pert nose and big brown eyes that forever danced merrily. She was dressed in a burnt-orange chiffon pants suit and looked decidedly delectable. Standing next to her, Ben looked even taller than his six feet and very handsome in the pale blue suit that matched his eyes. A wildly patterned silk shirt in varying shades of blue set off his ruddy good looks and shock of sandy-colored hair.

Babs's eyes went over Sam slowly, taking in the combination of green gown, red hair, and flawless skin. Brown eyes laughing, she gave a small pout.

"Oh, Sam! Any woman that looks as gorgeous as you should be outlawed."

CHAPTER 2

What a night! They had dinner and Babs did some gambling at the M.G.M. but she would not stay in one place. They hit the Sands, Caesars, and other casinos, and while Babs and Ben stood at the tables or played blackjack Sam wandered through the rooms. Sam didn't gamble, but she assured her friends she was completely happy just watching. And watch she did. She was fascinated. She had been to all the posh casinos in Europe but never had she seen anything like this. The magnificence of the decor in the different hotels was worth seeing, but what absorbed Sam were the people. All kinds of people, from all over the world, from the very elegantly dressed to the almost (but not quite) down at heel. Many looked to Sam as if they hadn't slept for days, and the very air seemed to be charged with the excitement of a living thing.

Except for a light tinge of color in her cheeks and an added sparkle in her green eyes, Sam looked as always as she drifted in and out of the rooms—cool, composed, her bearing almost regal. And in a town full of almost unbelievably beautiful women, eyes followed Sam wherever she went. Male eyes avidly; female, enviously.

She had a wonderful time and when Ben announced that they must leave, she was surprised to see it was light outside. They dashed into the M.G.M. to get their valises, change and then taxied to the airport. Within an hour Ben was circling Vegas and heading the Piper toward home, and Babs was strapped into her seat fast asleep. It was a short flight and soon they were at the house.

Sam exclaimed her delight over the large, rambling ranch house set in beautifully landscaped grounds, as Ben grinned at her. "Our mine might not be as grand as the Ruth, but it keeps the wolf from the door." Sam grinned back. She knew that copper was not the only thing Ben's family had, but timber and cattle, and different industries as well.

The house was designed in a U-shape with hallways leading off the large foyer. Babs linked arms with Sam, leading her down the hall to their left to a large airy room, one wall of which was practically all glass. Sam looked around at the light Danish furniture, the deep rose carpet, pale pink walls, and scarlet draperies drawn open at the wall. "What a lovely room, Babs," she murmured, walking to the glass wall to gaze out at what was obviously the back of the house. A beautiful lawn dotted with shrubbery and trees in early soft green bud, due to the unseasonally warm weather, greeted her eyes. At the base of the lawn to her left was a kidney-shaped pool with a patio surrounding it and across from it to Sam's right was a tennis court. Also to Sam's right but closer to the house sat several umbrellaed tables with lawn chairs placed around them. Altogether it was a lovely view. Sam turned back to Babs with a soft smile. "You have a beautiful home, Babs."

Babs nodded in agreement, obviously pleased. "Now come see the most beautiful of all." She led Sam back along the hall near the end where Sam surmised the family bedrooms were and into the nursery. A young girl approximately seventeen sat in a rocking chair, reading to a

25

chubby, towheaded toddler and Sam could see an infant asleep in a crib against the wall. On seeing Babs, the boy cried "Mommy," slid off the girl's lap, and ran into Babs's arms. She swung him up to her, turning to Sam, "Benjie, this is your Aunt Sam," and to Sam proudly, "Ben, Jr." Sam took a chubby little hand into her own, smiled, and said quietly. "Hello, Ben, Jr. I hope you and I will be great friends."

Benjie stared at her with huge brown eyes a moment, then a beautiful smile breaking his face, he stretched out his arms to her, gurgling, "An Sam."

Laughing, Sam took him into her arms, enjoying his sweet, clean smell, while Babs looked on proud and delighted at her son's easy conquest.

"A charmer, just like his father." A voice came from the doorway, and Sam glanced up to see Ben, his face reflecting his wife's pride.

"He certainly is," Sam laughed. Her eyes went back to Benjie. "Would you like to show me your new brother?" He nodded; his face becoming eager as he turned in Sam's arms and pointed a small finger at the crib. Sam walked to the crib and looked down at the small duplicate of the child in her arms. Before she could say anything, Benjie's small finger moved to his lips and he whispered, "Baby seep." Laughing softly, Sam turned to a beaming Babs, "I envy you." It was not a casual compliment, it was true. Sam had felt a shaft of pure envy go through her as she gazed at the sleeping child, and had felt surprised and slightly shocked. Never being around small children much, she had never experienced their enslaving charm. She was completely captured.

Babs smiled at the young girl who was now standing by the rocking chair. "And this is Judy Demillo, my housekeeper's daughter and the baby's nursemaid, among other things. Please be very nice to her, for we must keep her happy." She grinned teasingly. "I could not possibly cope without her."

While Babs was speaking, Sam studied the girl. She was a beauty, very slender, with dark hair and brows and big dark eyes set in a thin, heartshaped face. Her skin had a creamy magnolia texture that was probably the envy of all her friends.

"Hello, Judy," Sam extended her hand, smiling gently, thinking the girl had the look of a timid doe.

"How do you do, Miss Denning." Judy returned Sam's smile shyly. Her small hand was as soft as a baby's, her voice was light, sweet. "Shall I take Benjie now?" Sam gave the boy a quick hug before handing him to Judy.

"I want a shower before lunch," Babs declared, turning toward the door. "And I imagine you do too, Sam." As they left the room Sam smiled at Judy and blew a kiss to Benjie from her fingertips.

Back in the hall Babs went to a door directly across from the nursery. "Lunch in two hours, Sam, and don't fuss. Wear jeans or whatever you're comfortable in. I'll come for you a few minutes early and show you around the house."

Babs knocked on Sam's door an hour and a half later. Sam had unpacked her suitcases, had a quick shower and a short nap, which had taken the edge off her tiredness. Now, dressed in pale-green denim slacks and a hunter-green ribbed pullover, her face devoid of makeup, she looked lovely, if a little pale. Babs had a slightly drawn look herself. She was in blue jeans and a white knit top, which stole all color from her face. She had a fuzzy look around her eyes, which told Sam she had also had a nap. "I'm not used to the night life anymore." Babs laughed tiredly. "I think I'd better have another nap before dinner,

27

if I don't want to fall asleep at the table." As they strolled down the hall, Sam yawned, then grinned apologetically. "I think I'd better do the same."

Sam loved the rambling house. As they went from room to room she noted that the keynote here was comfort. The furnishings were expensive, but casual, and some pieces, Sam's practiced eye told her, were priceless. Yet everything blended perfectly, giving the house a warm, relaxed atmosphere. The contrast between it and the elegant house in Long Island was astonishing. Again Sam felt that odd twinge in her chest, thinking, this is a home for a family, a house for raising children and sharing love, a reflection of the contentment Babs and Ben shared.

Babs saved the kitchen for last. Although Sam's love of cooking would greatly surprise anyone who knew her, other than her own family, Babs knew of it better than any other person. She had followed in Sam's wake into the kitchens of private homes and restaurants for years, standing back, watching Sam beguile and coax recipes from master cooks and chefs. Babs knew of the notebooks full of recipes Sam had collected from all over Europe. Now she watched, a smile on her lips, as Sam stood entranced in the middle of the large, spotlessly clean, fully equipped room. She led her to the small, slim, dark-haired woman preparing lunch at the stove.

"Sam, this is my housekeeper Marie Demillo."

"How do you do," Sam smiled, looking closely at Marie. "I see where Judy's beauty came from."

"Thank you, Miss Denning," Marie beamed. They chatted a few moments, Sam voicing appreciation of the well-kept kitchen, Marie appreciating Sam's appreciation. Lunch was a slow, relaxed affair, Sam and Ben bantering back and forth like longtime friends. Babs smiled contentedly. The man she loved and the friend she had always adored were fast friends. She was completely happy.

They had their coffee in the living room sitting comfortably in the big roomy chairs. Babs, glancing at her husband, murmured lazily. "When can we expect Morgan, darling?"

"I talked to him while you had your nap, and he said to tell you he promised to be here for dinner."

"I don't believe it!" she exclaimed. "Then he'll be here a few days with us. That man could certainly do with a rest." As Ben nodded, Babs caught the look of mild inquiry on Sam's face. "Ben's best friend, Morgan Wade," She explained. "He'll be godfather to your godmother for Mark. As a matter of fact, he's Benjie's godfather too." She paused a moment before chiding, "Come to think of it, you'd be Benjie's godmother, too, if you hadn't been traipsing around Vancouver or wherever at the time."

"I'm sorry now that I was away." Sam grinned at Babs. "I would have loved to have been Benjie's godmother." Searching her memory, she frowned. "Morgan Wade, the name sounds familiar, have I met him?"

"No, I don't think so," Babs mused. "Of course not, he was to be Ben's best man but he couldn't get here in time for the wedding, remember?"

Sam smiled and nodded but thought grimly, *Some wretched friend if he couldn't have made a better effort at the time, considering the swiftness of air travel.* She had thought the same at the time of the wedding, but then, as now, said nothing.

Ben leaned forward offering cigarettes to the women and after he lit them, he said, "I hope you'll like Morg, Sam."

"Morg's like an older brother," Babs chimed in, then

lifted her eyebrows at Ben. "How old is he? Thirty-two, thirty-three?"

"Three," Ben replied, and went on, laughter in his voice, "I dogged his feet like a puppy while I was growing up."

Sam's eyebrows went up in question. Babs supplied the answer. "Morg's a cattleman, has an immense spread upstate. His ancestors were headed for California, got as far as Nevada, and liked what they saw. They settled and the Wade spread has been here ever since. All of them cattlemen, till Morg's father, George. He was a maverick. A friend got him interested in photography while he was still a teen-ager and he was lost to ranching forever."

Ben took up the narrative. "The ranch came to him when Morg was about fourteen, and he installed a manager, allowing himself freedom to accept assignments all over the world, mostly wildlife. As he and my father were close friends, Morg came to us whenever George took on a new assignment. He was with us through most of his teens, seeing his father only at holidays and summer vacation."

"And he's a throwback." Babs laughed. "A cattleman to the core. He loves that spread with a passion. Hates to leave it, that's why I was surprised when Ben said he'll be here today, three days before time. I wouldn't have been at all surprised if he'd have arrived Sunday morning, just in time to go to the church."

Ben lay back in his chair, his legs stretched out, his eyes looking back on memories.

"Old Morg even tried to opt out of college," he reminisced, "but his father finally convinced him that a well-rounded education was necessary, even to a rancher. He worked like hell during his college years, went every summer, did the work of four years in three and still graduated

30

near the top of his class. His father died in Africa of one of those rare things we'd never even heard of while Morgan was in his senior year. Then it was my father who had to talk to him like a Dutch uncle to keep him in school."

Babs again took up the story. "As it turned out, the manager George had hired had not been a good one. When Morgan came home from school at age twenty-one, he found the ranch run down and finances fairly well depleted. And he's been working like a fiend the last twelve years to build it up again. Practically lives on the land, being in the house just about long enough to eat and sleep, if that. Even though he has the best housekeeper this side of St. Louis."

"I don't believe that." They were the first words Sam had uttered in the last half hour.

"Oh, but it's true," Babs laughed, "and Marie would be the first one to tell you that Sara Weaver is a gold mine. She came out here from the Pennsylvania Dutch country with Morgan's mother, Betty, when she married George. And as Betty died in a car accident when Morgan was two, Sara is the closest thing to a mother Morg has ever known." She glanced at Ben. "Except maybe your mother."

Ben nodded. "Yes, Morg's fond of Mother but he was in his teens when he came to us and by then he was Sara's."

"She must have missed him during those years," Sam put in, and again Ben nodded. "And I know he missed her. When he finally came home to stay, even with the money so tight, he re-did the ranch house for her."

Babs piped in, "You should see his kitchen, Sam, it'd blow your mind."

Sam stared at her in disbelief, this from a woman whose

31

kitchen would blow any cook's mind. Babs laughed gaily and held up one hand.

"Honest injun, it's something else. Marie turns green at the mention of it."

"Then I shan't mention it," Sam promised softly. Babs stood up, stretching and yawning. "I'm going to spend some time with the kids before I go for another nap. Want to join me, Sam?"

"I certainly do," came the reply from an equally drowsy Sam. As they left the room they both smiled fondly at Ben, already half asleep in his chair.

They spent the next hour in the nursery and Sam was given the honor of feeding Mark his bottle. As she held the tiny baby in her arms, Sam again experienced that small shaft of envy. He was so small, so very beautiful, and for the first time in her life Sam wondered what it would be like to have a child of her own. When the boys were put down for their naps, Sam and Babs made for their own beds.

In her room Sam drew the scarlet draperies over the glass wall, pulled her top over her head, then slid out of her sandals and slacks. Stretching out on the bed in her bikini panties and bra, she was instantly asleep. The late afternoon sunrays, the glare muted by the draperies, crawled up the bed, waking Sam when they touched her face. She glanced at the clock by the bed quickly, remembering Babs's parting words: "Dinner at eight, cocktails in the living room at seven thirty."

It was not quite six, so Sam lazed another half hour, not quite asleep yet not fully awake, before she rose to get ready for dinner. She had a long, warm bath, the water scented with salts, and as she soaked she wondered idly what Ben's friend would be like. Shrugging her shoulders carelessly, she stepped out of the tub, patted herself dry, slipped into a lacy bra and briefs and made her face up lightly. After dropping a hot-pink, raw silk caftan over her head, she slid her feet into soft leather sandals while she pulled the pins from her hair, thinking she should have removed them before lying down as her scalp was smarting at spots from their digging in. As she brushed her hair, she decided to wear it loose this evening to let her scalp heal. Giving one last flick with the brush, she looked into the mirror, decided she'd do, and left the room.

Although it was past seven thirty when she entered the living room, she found it empty, and hesitating only a moment, she made for the kitchen, pausing in the doorway to ask, "May I come in, Marie?"

"Of course, Miss Denning," came the reply from Marie, standing at the sink washing vegetables.

"Sam."

"Miss Sam," Marie emphasized.

"Done." Sam walked across the room to stand looking down over Marie's shoulder and added, her voice eager as a child's, "What's for dinner?"

Marie turned a smiling face up to Sam, "Mr. Morgan's a steak man, so I'm broiling Delmonicos on the charcoal grill outside. The foil-wrapped potatoes have been in the coals for an hour already. With that you'll have broccoli hollandaise and a tossed salad."

"Dressing?"

"My own."

"Hmmm, I can't wait," Sam laughed. "And dessert?"

"We'll let that be a surprise."

"Sounds super." Sam smiled, retracing her steps out of the kitchen. She heard voices as she neared the doorway to the living room. On entering, she paused and three heads were turned toward her. For a few moments she had the unreal feeling of a stop-motion effect and was unaware

33

of the picture she made, framed in the doorway. The moment was broken as she stepped out of the frame into the room, and at the same time the three people came to their feet out of their chairs.

Babs walked over to Sam, a vision in teal-blue chiffon, her voice teasing, "We had just decided you were still asleep, and I was delegated to go tip the bed." Sam shook her head lightly and replied softly, "I was in the kitchen with Marie."

"I should have known," Babs laughed.

In the few seconds that this exchange lasted, Sam was sizing up the man standing beside Ben. He was, she judged, at least six feet two inches, perhaps six feet three inches tall. Broad-shouldered, narrow-hipped, long-legged, and slim almost to the point of gauntness. Feeling the short hairs on her nape bristle, Sam thought, *That's the most dangerous-looking male animal I've ever seen.* On the heels of that thought she felt a tiny curl in her stomach which she recognized, in some shock, as fear. Fear? Then she was standing in front of him, hearing Babs say simply, "Samantha Denning—Morgan Wade."

Lifting her eyes, Sam was struck, as if from an actual blow, by the direct, riveting stare from the coldest black eyes she had ever seen.

It seemed the curl grew inside her as she automatically answered "Mr. Wade" to his "Miss Denning," spoken in a disturbingly soft voice. She was fighting an alien sense of panic, his eyes still on her, as she nodded yes to Ben's "Martini, Sam?" The eye contact was broken when Morgan turned to Ben's query to refill his glass, and Sam sank thankfully into a chair.

Sam sat very straight, almost rigid, on the edge of her chair, her face composed, if somewhat pale, showing nothing of the turmoil in her mind. With growing amazement, she wondered at her reaction to this man. Instant dislike she'd have understood. She had experienced that at times. But fear? Yes, a very real, if small, jolt of fear. That she had never experienced before. It was almost as if, in some way, he was a threat to her. She heard Babs's chatting and smiled in her direction. What was she talking about? Sam hadn't the vaguest idea. When Morgan turned back to her to hand her her drink, Sam saw his eyes glitter briefly at her barely whispered "thank you." Hearing the slight tremor in her own voice, she mentally pulled herself up short thinking, enough of this nonsense. Feeling a slow anger beginning to burn inside, she lifted her chin. As she did, black eyes again struck hers, but this time the glance bounced off eyes as cold, as hard as the emerald they matched in color. And as the sun strikes sparks from the stone, her glance struck sparks of challenge. She saw his own glint in acceptance. She had thrown the glove. He had picked it up.

Warfare silently declared, voices slowly penetrated. Something was being said on their roles at the christening, and she made herself relax against the back of the chair, hearing Babs say, "Okay with you, Sam?" Again she smiled and nodded. She would have to question Babs later on this point. Was what okay with her? Sam hadn't the least clue.

Ben asked Morgan Wade something about the ranch, and the conversation switched to ranching in general. Putting a look of interest on her face, Sam sipped at her drink and studied him over the rim of her glass.

He sat lazily in his chair, his long legs stretched out, crossed at the ankles. His arms formed a triangle, elbows on the chair arms, holding his drink with both hands in front of him. His hands were big, the fingers long and slender, and Sam felt a small shiver skip down her spine on seeing his right index finger rub and caress the rim of his glass. She shifted her gaze to his clothes—a lightweight suit, expensive, in a rich brown that almost matched his skin color, with a pale yellow shirt open at the throat, the sight of which also disturbed her vaguely.

Again her gaze shifted, upward, to his face, not quite in profile as he looked at Ben, who was speaking. Decidedly good-looking, almost devastatingly so, saved from being handsome by the almost harsh bone structure. The jaw firm, hard, the nose longish, but straight, well-defined, hard lips, the cheeks high, and overall the brown skin stretched tight, smooth, with shallow hollows under the cheekbones adding to the look of gauntness. Hair as black as his eyes, thick and wiry, growing a little long to curl at the collar and behind the ears. Full black eyebrows, with a slight arch, and the longest, thickest black eyelashes Sam had ever seen on a man.

Babs interrupted the men's talk with "Dinner, bring your drinks" and they drifted into the dining room. It was a disaster. Sam found herself sitting directly across the table from Morgan and every time he spoke, whether to her or to the others, she felt her anger and resentment grow. It wasn't what he said, but the tone in which he said it. In fact, she was hard put to remember what was said all evening. She only knew that by the end of it, she had labeled Morgan Wade as that blasted arrogant cowboy.

She tried to do justice to Marie's dinner, but only pushed it around on her plate with her fork. The surprise dessert, which turned out to be an exceptional mousse, she barely touched. When Babs questioned her on it, she pleaded fatigue for the loss of her appetite. Having done so, she used fatigue again to excuse herself shortly after they had finished their coffee in the living room. There was no demur, but she caught the arched brow and mocking look Morgan gave her as he wished her a quiet good night. In her room she thought in agitation she would be unable to sleep, but she fell asleep at once.

Sam wakened to bright, spring sunshine and a feeling of well being. Stretching in contentment, she laughed and chided herself on her feelings of the night before, telling herself, he's a man like every other, a little full of his own importance, but certainly no threat to her. She would make an effort to be pleasant in the face of his arrogance and in four days time they would both be gone. He to his ranch, and she to Long Island.

That settled, she had a shower, dressed quickly in flat sandals, jeans, and a pullover. She brushed her hair, pulled it back, twisted it, and pinned it to her head with a long barrette. Feeling famished, she left her room in search of breakfast. She found Babs alone at the breakfast table, and was informed that Ben and Morgan had left an hour ago on business of their own. The knowledge dismayed her not at all. The morning passed swiftly. Sam made periodic trips to the nursery, falling more in love with the two boys every time.

The men were back for lunch, and Sam felt relief as Babs again ran over the procedure to be followed at the church two days hence. Sam, changing the conversation, determined to stick to her earlier resolve, told Ben and Morgan what she and Babs had done all morning, and in turn, asked what they had been up to.

Morgan cast her a quick, surprised look, a question in his eyes then, as if he understood her purpose and agreed with it, he answered her, his voice deep and pleasant. Sam almost sighed audibly in relief. Maybe, just maybe, they would get through the next few days without coming to blows.

They again took their coffee into the living room, the

men following slowly behind the women. Sam was already seated when they strolled into the room and as she glanced up, her breath caught at the appearance Morgan made. His slim length alone was arresting. He was wearing a white cotton shirt that was a glare against his dark skin as he walked through a ray of sunlight shining into the room from the french doors. The shirt was tucked into skin-tight jeans that rode low on his hips and across his stomach, which was not just flat but almost concave, causing his belt buckle to tilt forward slightly at the top. Both men were in stocking feet, as they had been riding and had removed their boots before entering the house.

After their second cup of coffee the men excused themselves, claiming work and Babs, drawing her mouth into a mock pout, complained of being neglected. The pout changed to delighted laughter as Morgan, passing her chair, reached down and ruffled her hair. "There isn't a man alive who could neglect you, gorgeous," he drawled as he sauntered from the room, his entire form a picture of unconscious grace. Sam moved uneasily in her chair.

Babs turned to her, laughter still in her voice. "What a charming liar that man is." The tone of her voice told Sam the deep affection she had for him. Sam resolved again to keep it light, she would in no way have Babs hurt.

Babs poured herself more coffee and settling back, cradled her cup in her palms with a sigh. "Well, finally, now we can have a long talk." She proceeded to inquire after Mary and Deb, asking if the wedding was still on for October and then, gently, of Sam's father's death. Sam answered her questions, then told her the details of her father's will.

Babs sat staring at her a moment, the look on her face one of sheer disbelief. After long seconds she exclaimed, "My God, Sam! That's pure Victorian."

"I know," Sam smiled. "I had exactly the same reaction."

"What are you going to do?" Babs asked as everyone else had who heard the conditions of the will.

"I haven't the foggiest, love," Sam said wryly. "I simply do not know."

"Unreal," Babs murmured, "positively unreal."

"Quite."

The subject was dropped as they decided to visit the boys. As they left the room, Babs's head still shook in wonder.

They had been with the boys perhaps an hour when Ben and Morgan came in. Sam had been sitting with Benjie, who, on seeing Morgan, slid off her lap to run toward him, little arms outstretched, shouting, "Unca Mog, Unca Mog." Bending down, Morgan caught the child under the arms, swung him off his feet, and tossed him into the air over his head, teasing. "What's up, hotshot?"

Sam caught her breath at the rough handling of the child, releasing it slowly when Benjie squealed, "Ben is," just as big hands seemed to pluck him out of the air. Benjie piped excitedly, "Again, again," but Morgan shook his head. "Not today, chum, let's have a look at your brother." Walking to the crib, Benjie repeated the words he'd said to Sam the day before, "Baby seep."

"Then we'll be very quiet," Morgan whispered as he reached the crib and stood looking down. Then, his voice tone normal, "Playing possum, he's wide awake."

Sam drew her breath in sharply and held it as suddenly she saw his arm tighten around Benjie's small bottom and bending, slide the other arm under Mark. Straightening slowly he turned, the baby securely caught against him. Sam expelled her breath on a rush, hearing Babs laugh.

"It shook me the first time I saw him do it, too, Sam."

Morgan gave her a wicked grin, delighted in knowing he'd frightened her—twice. Still grinning, which made a lie of his words, he drawled mockingly, "I'm sorry if I shook you, Miss Denning."

Before Sam could retort, he turned to Judy, "Did I frighten you too, beautiful?"

Sam watched color stain Judy's cheeks thinking, *Babs is "Gorgeous," Judy's "Beautiful," and I'm Miss Denning, I guess that'll keep me in my place.*

"You couldn't frighten me, Morgan," Judy laughed, the color deepening in her face.

She's got a crush on him, Sam decided, watching the color mount in Judy's cheeks. Shifting her gaze, she studied Morgan's smiling face, his teasing eyes. This one, she thought, is used to female adoration—very used to it. For some strange reason the thought was unsettling.

A short time later Babs announced, "Nap time." To Benjie's cried "not yet" Morgan replied in mock sternness, "Sack out, wrangler," and handed him to Judy and Mark to Babs. Kisses were given and received, and Sam, Ben, and Morgan left the room, Babs calling, "I'll be out in a minute."

Sam headed for her room but was stopped by Ben's invitation. "Come have a drink, Sam." She hesitated, but then followed them into the living room.

Ben started for the liquor cabinet but was stopped by Morgan's hand on his arm. "Sit, I'll get it." Without asking, he mixed two Martinis, turning to hand one to Sam and place the other at Babs's usual chair. Then taking two more glasses he put an ice cube into each, filled the glasses halfway with Jack Daniel's, and handed one to Ben. Moving to stand in front of the fireplace, he took a long, appreciative swallow of his whiskey.

Babs came into the room, dropped into her chair,

picked up her drink, sipped, and murmured, "Hmm good. Benjie's a love, isn't he?" She asked the room in general, which brought a laugh from them all. The talk was light and easy for a time. Then, refilling his glass, Morgan moved to the doorway with a casual "I'm for a bath." Ben soon followed, claiming a nap wouldn't hurt either.

Sam and Babs sat quietly for a time, sipping their drinks. Suddenly Babs sat up, looked at Sam with an odd expression on her face and exclaimed. "Of course! That's the answer, Sam, Morgan."

"Whatever are you talking about?" Sam asked lazily.

"You can marry Morgan," came the jolting reply. Sam's eyes flew wide, and her voice rose slightly.

"Have you gone mad?"

"Not yet," Babs answered serenely. "It's the perfect solution to the will, Sam."

"Really Babs?" Sam began. "But I don't see . . ."

"Of course it is, Sam," Babs interrupted. "You need a husband within five months, right?" Sam nodded. "Yet you have no wish to marry any of the men who have already offered." The nod was more emphatic. "You think they'd want a regular marriage? A normal male–female relationship?"

"I know they would."

"Okay," Babs went on. "You get a husband. No demands. Morgan gets a wife with money, which he needs."

"It couldn't work," Sam stately firmly. "In the first place I hardly know the man." She held up her hand as Babs started to interrupt. "And in the second place, although he may need money, he doesn't strike me as needing a wife overmuch."

"That's where you're wrong," Babs denied. "He can hardly step off the place but that the females are falling all over him, trying to drag him down the aisle. And he is

41

simply not interested. Oh, he's had his flings, as a matter of fact quite a few, but he is too wrapped up in that ranch to be bothered with a wife."

"But then why do you think . . ."

"That's the beauty of it, Sam. This way, with a wife, he gets a modicum of immunity from the felines, without the demands of a more, er, normal marriage. And what does your barely knowing him have to do with it? Will you think, Sam? You could use the house, a place he spends very little time in, as a home base and travel around to wherever you please. As long as you touch home for a short stay occasionally, in this day and age, who could call that a separation?"

She paused to draw breath, but before Sam could say anything Babs went on. "At the end of five years, you get a quiet divorce and go your separate ways. Morgan financially in the black at last and you with, I'm sure, the bulk of your inheritance intact."

"Oh, Babs, I don't know, you make it sound as if it almost might do."

"What else is there?" Babs insisted. "It would be lovely if you could fall in love, but really, Sam, if in all these years you haven't met Prince Charming, I somehow can't see him tooling down the pike in his Maserati within the next few months." Babs grinned impishly at her.

Sam grinned back. "I can't either, but, good God, how would one go about it? I mean really, one can't just walk up to a comparative stranger and declare, 'I say, would you care to marry me for my money?' "

Babs giggled and Sam had to smile, but added, "I mean it, Babs, I couldn't do it."

"You don't have to," Babs told her, "I'll explain to Ben and he'll talk to Morgan."

"Do you really think?"

"I do."

Sam hesitated long moments, then sighed. "All right, I don't like it, but I don't see any other way short of sponging off Mary."

Babs knew that was the deciding factor.

CHAPTER 3

As she dressed for dinner, Sam felt nervous to the point of being sick. She should not have told Babs to go ahead. If that arrogant cowboy mocked her offer, she'd leave at once for Long Island, christening or no christening. No, she'd hit him first, then she'd leave.

She had made up her face carefully and now, standing in front of the closet, she decided, since the evening was cool, to wear a longsleeved hostess gown in apple green. Cut like a shirtwaist, it clung snugly at the top, tapering to the small, belted waist, the skirt hanging in full soft folds to the floor. Giving herself a last glance in her full-length mirror, she lifted her shoulders in resignation, then left the room.

Dinner went smoothly, Ben and Morgan carrying most of the conversation, discussing the merits of different breeds of cattle, much to the disdain of Babs. For her part, Sam was happy to remain quiet and concentrate on forcing her food down. Back in the living room, with coffee cups in hand, the talk centered on various activities of their mutual friends. As soon as Morgan had set his cup down, Ben excused the both of them, to a surprised look from Morgan, and they again left the room.

Sam got up and circled the room, only to sit down again with a sigh, upon which Babs shot her a look and stated firmly, "We need a drink." Babs then proceeded to make a pitcherful of Martinis. She poured out two and handed one to Sam, who downed it in four fast swallows.

"Good grief, Sam, relax. You do much more of that and you'll be flat on the floor."

Sam shrugged and refilled her glass, but she sat back into her chair, drawing her feet under her, and sipped at the drink. Babs launched into a discussion of clothes and from there to her children. The time seemed to drag and Sam, pouring her third drink, was beginning to fidget when they heard the men returning.

Morgan went directly to the Jack Daniel's, but Ben stopped inside the doorway saying softly, "I think Benjie is calling for us, Babs." Babs literally jumped out of her chair, glanced at Sam, and left, Ben right behind her.

Sam sipped her drink watching Morgan warily. He dropped the cube into the glass, then splashed the whiskey over it and turned. As he walked slowly to Sam, she had the urge to run, and kept her seat out of sheer will power. Morgan was wearing a white denim suit with a patterned shirt in shades of blue, and he looked completely at ease. He stopped a few feet from her, still silent. His eyes on her, he lifted his glass and took a long swallow. She could tell nothing from his face or eyes and was having trouble keeping her fingers from trembling, when he lowered the glass. His soft tone sent a shiver down her arms. "I hear you want to make a trade."

"A trade?" she whispered, thinking she sounded rather stupid.

He gave a short nod and stated bluntly, "My name for your money." She bristled, but forced herself to answer, "Yes."

"When?"

"Why, I don't know, there's my family and . . ." she faltered.

"No, as soon as legally possible," he cut in adamantly.

"But, really—" she began, but he cut her off again.

"I want to get back to the ranch, and do you really want your family here? How long do you think it would take them to get wise? Better to let them think you've had a whirlwind affair that ended at the altar. Right?"

"I suppose so."

"Good. Bargain?"

"Bargain," Sam answered weakly.

"Okay," he said briskly. "Tomorrow we'll go into town and apply for a license and do whatever else has to be done. Then as soon as we can, we'll get married and go home."

"Whatever you say," Sam murmured faintly, wondering if she was going to be sick as she gulped at her drink.

At that moment Babs stuck her head around the doorway. "All right if we come in?"

Morgan laughed, white teeth flashing in his dark face. "Of course, it's your house."

They talked for over an hour, Ben and Babs advising them on what must be done. Then Sam rose, stating, "If we're having an early start, I think I'll turn in," and left the room quickly. Babs caught up to her in the hallway outside her room and putting her hand on Sam's arm whispered, "Are you all right, Sam?"

"Of course," Sam assured her. "It's just . . . everything's happening so fast."

"I know, but I think it'll work, really," Babs urged.

"I hope so." But Sam's voice didn't sound very hopeful.

The next three days blurred together for Sam. She woke Saturday morning tense and headachy, telling herself she couldn't go through with it, she'd have to beg off somehow. The headache and most of the tension drained away under a shower. Calmer now as she dressed, she thought hopefully, *Perhaps Morgan is having second thoughts.* It may be quite easy to call it off. They might even joke about it.

She stepped out of her room to see Morgan closing the door of his own directly across the hall, next to the nursery. Before she could open her mouth and without even a good morning he said almost curtly, "I was just going to knock on your door, breakfast is ready. Ben and Babs just sat down." Glancing at his watch impatiently he went on, "We better get moving."

"Mr. Wade," Sam started, but he broke in dryly.

"Don't you think you'd better call me Morgan, Samantha? The days of a wife calling her husband mister are long gone." Taking her arm he propelled her down the hall to the dining room, she practically running to keep up with his long-legged stride. She was breathing quickly when she reached the table and not only from the trip down the hall. She was emotionally shaken as well. Her only clear thought being, *I'm not going to be able to stop this.* With a rising sense of unease she turned to Babs, who had just wished her good morning, ready to plead, you've got to get me out of this. Babs, not waiting for Sam's return greeting, went on. "We're going into Ely with you. Ben has some things to look to, and unless you have a white dress with you, you and I have some shopping to do."

"A white dress! What for?" Sam repeated in surprise, catching the quick, sharp-eyed look Morgan threw at her.

"What for?" Now it was Babs's turn to repeat. "Why, to get married in, silly. Do you have one with you?"

Before Sam could answer, Ben, laughing softly, said, "I don't think our bride is altogether awake yet." Thinking *I don't think your bride's all together, period,* Sam an-

47

swered Babs, "No, I don't have one, but I don't think it necessary to wear white." Morgan and Babs spoke simultaneously.

"I don't see why not."

"Of course it is."

"But . . ." Sam started.

"Samantha," Morgan interrupted sharply, "I know I said I'd like to do this as fast as possible, but I didn't mean we shouldn't do it right."

"Exactly," Babs stated firmly.

Sam's hands fluttered, turning palms out, and she gave in with a barely audible, "All right, we'll shop." Taking a roll from the bun warmer in the middle of the table, she sat crumbling it onto her plate. Feeling Morgan's eyes watching her, she glanced up.

"You'd better have some breakfast."

"I'm n-not really h-hungry," she stammered. Blast it, she'd never stammered in her life. "Coffee and juice will do."

"Then drink your juice," he ordered. Picking up the coffee carafe, he filled her cup and then the mug in front of him.

Anger burned through her at the tone of his voice. As if he were speaking to a child! She emptied the juice glass and placed it carefully on the table, observing coldly, "You're not eating."

At her words he cocked an eyebrow and smiled mockingly. "I ate over an hour ago. Unused to the good life, I get up early."

Babs chuckled. The burn deepening inside her, Sam turned and watched, in some disgust, as Babs polished off her bacon and eggs with sickening gusto.

Ben had already cleaned his plate and had just lit a cigarette. Turning to him, Sam asked, "May I have one, please?" Before Ben could reach for one, Morgan was holding his pack across the table. She took one, watched as he placed one between his teeth. His lighter flared, was touched to first hers then his cigarette. Teeth still clamped to the filtered end, he drawled, "Now drink your coffee so we can get moving."

Sam's green eyes flashed, but she emptied her cup. Crushing out the half-smoked cigarette, she left the table, hurried to her room, brushed her teeth, applied a light coat of lipstick to her mouth, grabbed her handbag, and joined the others, who were waiting for her beside a very dusty Buick station wagon parked in the driveway. Settling herself onto the back seat beside Babs, Sam could barely keep her nose from wrinkling. The inside of the car was every bit as dusty as the outside. At that moment Morgan slid behind the wheel and caught her reflection in the rearview mirror. As if he read her mind he drawled, "May as well have the heap washed while we're in Ely."

The heap being all of six months old, Sam had to assume he referred to all vehicles as heaps. Pulling her eyes from his mocking black ones, she stared sightlessly out of the window. The drive into Ely didn't take long enough for Sam. In fact none of the things they had to do seemed to take long. From filling out the marriage license form to speaking with Babs's pastor and arranging to have him marry them in his study on Wednesday morning at ten. Babs had insisted on the last, stating emphatically that a dusty civil office just would not do. With a mounting feeling of having won the battle but lost the war, Sam went along with everything decided, voicing no preference.

They separated, agreeing to meet again in two hours time for a late lunch; the women to shop, the men to follow their own pursuits, the nature of which Sam hadn't the vaguest idea. Except of course, the cleaning of the Buick.

Sam did not buy a dress. She found nothing she liked, admitting to Babs the fault was not in the shops or the merchandise. They had seen some lovely things. She was, as she told Babs, simply not with it. She shopped for the boys instead, to voiced disapproval from Babs.

Joining up with the men again, they entered a small coffeeshop. Morgan and Ben chose a booth and sat across the table from Sam and Babs. After giving their order of four cheeseburgers and coffees to the waitress, Babs told the men of the failure of the shopping trip.

Ben laughed, giving his wife a fond, teasing look. "Somehow that doesn't surprise me. I don't know a woman who can suit herself shopping inside two hours." Babs made a face at him but didn't answer. Sam, glancing up at Morgan, gave a small sigh. He wasn't laughing. Quite the opposite, his face had gone still, his mouth a hard, straight line. He sat silent while the waitress served their meal but as soon as she had walked away, he spoke to Ben, his eyes steady on Sam's face.

"May I use your plane Monday?"

"Certainly," came the prompt reply from Ben around a mouthful of burger, "Where are you headed?"

"Vegas. I'll fly the girls in early in the morning and Sam may take the day to shop. Hopefully she can suit herself there." This last on a decidedly mocking note.

Sam nearly choked on her burger and was about to protest, but catching the danger signals flashing from Morgan's eyes, changed her mind, thinking she could veto the plan later. Babs disabused her of that thought almost at once. "Oh, Sam, what luck, two trips to Vegas in the same week." Sam managed to give Babs a weak smile, then turned to frown at Morgan thinking, *All right, your point again, cowboy, but I swear I'll buy the first damned white dress my eyes land on, even if the wretched thing's a rag.*

They left the coffeeshop and made their way to the car which, Sam discovered, minus its coat of dust, was a lovely deep green. On the way back to the house Sam and Babs managed a half-hearted conversation, and once there, they went directly into the boys' room. Benjie squealed with delight at Sam's presents.

Sunday flew by for Sam. She was up early, helping Marie with the last-minute preparations for the buffet lunch to be served to the relatives and friends Babs had invited to the christening celebration. Then it was time to leave for the church. Sam held Mark throughout the service, he sleeping contently through it all. They drove directly back to the house, a long line of cars behind them.

Confusion reigned. The guests overflowed the house. Sam, silently giving thanks for the fair, mild weather, kept on the move. Steering clear of Morgan, she circulated, being greeted like a long-lost daughter by Babs's parents and younger sister, getting reacquainted with Ben's parents, and stopping to talk and laugh with people she had met at Babs and Ben's wedding. If she came upon a group that included Morgan at the time, she went right on by, but she was not unaware of the number of young, pretty females who seemed to hang on him, or of his deep, somewhat disturbing laughter that rang out frequently.

Sam had been on her feet, except for the time spent in church, for over sixteen hours and she had had too much champagne, she admitted to herself ruefully, when she sank gratefully onto her bed sometime after eleven. Pushing everything out of her mind she was asleep at once.

She woke slowly to a light tapping on the door. Before she could talk herself into moving, Babs poked her head inside, calling, "Wake up, sleepyhead, Morgan said to tell you to hit the deck, he wants to leave in an hour." On the verge of saying "Tell Morgan Wade to go to hell," the sight of Babs's happy, laughing face stopped her and she murmured, "Be with you in thirty minutes."

Grumbling to herself that he was some kind of flaming idiot, she showered and dressed in the pink pants suit she had flown west in. As she slid onto her chair at the table, she raised her eyebrows in question at the two empty places where Morgan and Ben usually sat.

Babs, sipping her coffee, her breakfast finished, stated, "They ate earlier. Ben's gone, had some people to see. Morg's changing his clothes, be with us in a minute."

"Aren't we the favored ones?" Sam purred acidly, attacking the dish of grapefruit in front of her, unaware of the quick, concerned look Babs gave her.

She was still jabbing listlessly at the fruit when Morgan strode into the room looking vital and alert in the white denim suit of a few nights ago, with a dark copper-colored shirt that, Sam grudgingly admitted to herself, looked terrific.

Without sitting, he poured himself coffee and stood drinking it, watching Sam quietly a few minutes before chiding softly, "No breakfast again." It was a statement, not a question. Sam, not bothering to answer or even look up, lay down her spoon, pushed her plate away, and lifted her cup to stare moodily at her coffee before sipping it.

Babs laughed a little nervously, knowing Sam's temper when aroused, and implored Morgan, "Have a care, Morg, Sam's still tired and a bit testy this morning."

Black eyes glinted with devilment and his tone was sardonic as he cooed, "Poor baby."

Sam jerked to her feet, her face a mask of cold hauteur.

"If we must have this shopping trip, then let's do so and have done with it."

The flight was too short for Sam's taste. She sat enjoying the panorama below her, occasionally asking questions of Babs, ignoring Morgan, which didn't seem to bother him in the least.

In Vegas they parted company, agreeing to meet for lunch. Sam did buy the first white dress she saw, simply because it was perfect—a sheath with long sheer sleeves and a cowl collar that stretched from one shoulder tip across her throat to the other, draping down the back revealing the upper half of her lovely shoulders and back. She chose soft white leather pumps and a large white leather bag against Babs's advice, who chided softly, "Don't you ever buy a handbag other than those huge ones?" Sam answered "never" shortly and declared herself outfitted, much to the delight of Babs, who decided to shop for herself as they still had an hour before meeting Morgan.

They left Vegas right after lunch, returning in time to play with Benjie before his nap. They idled the rest of the day away and Sam excused herself early to go to bed.

Sam's tension grew steadily Tuesday until, late in the afternoon, she had to force herself to laugh and reply lightly to Babs's concerned questioning.

"One doesn't get married every day, pet."

"I know," Babs replied, "But do you realize, Sam, you've barely spoken to Morgan for two days. I know this isn't a love match or anything, but you could try to be civil."

Chastising herself for her boorish behavior in her friends' home, Sam made an effort to hold her end of the conversation at dinner. Later in the evening, as she poured her fourth Martini, she decided she was running out of banalities when Morgan, stretched out lazily, rose to his feet in a fluid move, strolled across the room to her, and plucked her drink out of her hand.

"Walk outside with me for a while, there's something we have to discuss." Giving Babs and Ben a brief "excuse us," he led her from the room. He waited at the dining room for her to get a coat, then they went through the sliding glass doors in the dining room and onto the soft grass. He strolled toward the tennis courts and when he paused to light a cigarette for her and himself he said suddenly, his voice harsh, "What the hell are you trying to say with the booze?"

Caught off guard Sam stammered, "W-what?"

"Babs told me you're a very light drinker," he rasped. "Yet that drink I took from you was your fourth. Yesterday it was wine. As a matter of fact you've been belting it away since Friday. If you're having second thoughts, you don't have to drink yourself insensible, just say it and we'll drop the whole thing."

"I don't understand."

"I think you do. Do you want to call it off?"

"No, of course not," she answered quickly, too quickly.

"There's no *of course* about it," Morgan grated. "You better be sure, Samantha, very sure, before it becomes a fact. An irrevocable fact."

She thought his phrasing a bit odd, but again answered quickly, "I am."

He said nothing for some time, then, "All right, but let me suggest you lay off the booze and get some rest. We've got a long day tomorrow, starting early and ending late." Grasping her forearm in his big hand, he started back to the house.

Sam was speechless. Who did this man think he was? No one had ever presumed to tell her she had had too

54

much to drink or when to go to bed. Angry now, she snapped, "What do you think you're doing?" For, going through the dining room, he bypassed the living room, and was practically dragging her down the hall to her room. His fingers tightened painfully as she tried to stop and pull her arm free. She was shaking in fury when he stopped at the door to her room. Grasping her other arm he held her still and bending over her, said softly, "Calm down and stop acting like a spoiled child. You're so up-tight you're about ready to go off like a firecracker." His voice held laughter as he ended, "Get some sleep. You want to be a beautiful bride, don't you?"

"Oh, you—" Sam began, only to gasp as, dipping his head swiftly he brushed his lips across hers and whispered, "Good night, Samantha." Pushing open the door he gave her a gentle shove into the room and pulled the door closed firmly behind her.

Sam stood inside the door, still, rigid, her hands tightly fisted at her side. *I must be mad,* she thought wildly. *Why didn't I stop this when I had the chance? It can't possibly work, he has nothing but contempt for me and I hate him.* She was uncomfortably aware that her mouth tingled from that brief brush of his and her arms felt hot where his hands had held her. She felt a very real fear. *I must stop this,* she thought desperately.

But she didn't. It was over quickly. She stayed in her room until it was time to leave. Babs brought her coffee, which she drank, and toast, which she ignored. She dressed and paced the room until Morgan knocked on the door with a quiet, "It's time to go, Samantha." Sam hesitated, stepped back, then lifting her chin, walked to the door and opened it to stand straight and still as his eyes went over her body, then back to hers.

"You look lovely."

55

"Thank you." Her face was perfectly composed, her voice icy. She walked past him and down the hall to Babs, waiting at the door. The drive into town was uncomfortable, Morgan and Babs eyeing Sam warily. If someone had asked Sam to describe the pastor's study five minutes after leaving it, she would have been unable to do so. Yet the brief service was vividly imprinted on her mind. Morgan's voice, deep, firm, repeating, "With this ring I thee wed, with my body I thee worship, with all my worldly goods I thee endow," as he slid a narrow platinum band on her finger. Her own voice low but clear, repeating the same vows and placing a ring, the larger twin to her own, on his finger. The ring, hastily handed to her by Babs, was a complete surprise to Sam. Even as she slid it into place she could not believe he'd leave it there. He simply did not come across as the type of man who would advertise his marital status. But then, Sam still had a lot to learn about Morgan Wade.

When the pastor said, "You may kiss the bride," Morgan brushed her lips as he had the night before and then Babs and Ben kissed her. Minutes later they were back in the car. They went directly back to the house as Marie was preparing what she called a wedding luncheon for them. Ben drove and, as they had entered the back seat, Sam sat as close to the door panel as she could, giving a short nod, but not even looking up as Morgan said, "Excuse me," when he stretched his long legs across to her side of the floor, bumping her foot with his.

Without speaking, Sam sat staring out the window, seeing nothing, unaware that her fingers twisted at her ring, or of black eyes watching her, anger building in them. What she was aware of was the same tingling feeling on her mouth that she had felt the night before.

Marie and Judy were waiting to toast the newlyweds

with champagne when they returned to the house. Sam didn't know whether to laugh or cry, and she felt sorry for Judy, whose eyes, whenever they touched Morgan, grew sad and forlorn. Drawing Babs aside Sam asked, "Will there be time for me to call home before lunch?"

"Of course," Babs answered with a small laugh, as Benjie had joined the group and was jumping up and down in noisy excitement. "Use the phone in Ben's study, it'll be quiet there."

Sam entered the study, then turned in surprise as Morgan followed her into the room, closed the door and leaned back lazily against it. "I'd like some privacy, if you don't mind," she snapped.

"I do mind," he replied flatly. "I'm staying."

She glared at him, but he returned the look coolly, not moving. Turning her back to him sharply, she perched on the edge of Ben's desk, reached for the receiver, and dialed the Long Island number. Beth answered.

"This is Sam, Beth, is Mary about?" Then to Beth's inquiry of herself, "I'm fine. How are you?" Beth told Sam she was also fine, then asked her to hold on as she went in search of Mary. A few minutes later Sam heard Mary's gentle voice. "Hello, Samantha? Is something wrong, dear?"

Forcing her voice to lightness, Sam answered, "Not at all, just the opposite." Breathing deeply, she closed her eyes. "I was married this morning." Silence.

"Sam, are you joking?"

Sam, hearing the note of concern in Mary's voice, plunged on. "No, darling, I'm not joking, we just returned from the church a few minutes ago."

"But, my dear, who? Do I know him?"

"No, you don't know him, Mother. I just met him myself." She managed a light laugh. "Swept me off my feet. His name's Morgan Wade, a friend of Ben's, little Mark's godfather. He's a rancher here in Nevada," she added quickly before Mary could ask what he did.

"Sam, is this wise?" Mary's soft voice was tinged with suspicion.

"I don't know," Sam said gaily. "Is it ever? I don't much care, I'm in love." She was amazed she didn't choke.

"Are you truly?" Mary asked hopefully.

"Yes, Mother, truly," she affirmed, uncomfortably aware of Morgan leaning against the door.

She was not prepared for Mary's next question. "May I speak to him, Sam?" Without thinking, she turned a frantic face to him. As if he'd heard Mary's voice, Morgan walked across the room, and took the receiver from her hand. Sam was amazed at the gentleness of his tone.

"Hello, Mrs. Denning, this is Morgan."

Sam watched him as he listened and when he spoke again his voice was warm, seemingly sincere. "Yes, I know it was very fast. But I assure you it will be all right."

Again he listened then answered, "No, we can't come east just now. This is a very busy time for me at the ranch." There was a pause. "I appreciate that fact, and I promise you I'll bring Sam east as soon as I can. Yes, of course." Another pause, then, "Hello, yourself, how are you?" His tone was lighter and Sam knew he was now talking to Deb. She knew Deb's question had been, "How is Sam?" by his answer: "Sam's fine." His tone grew teasing, "In fact she's beautiful, isn't she?"

Oh, brother, Sam thought, his tongue should fall out of his head. She heard him say, "Of course you may," then he handed the receiver to her and walked back to the door.

Sam thought to forestall Deb's questions by saying, "Hello, Poppet, will you do a favor for me?"

"Of course, what is it?" Deb answered.

58

"Well, call the Messrs. Baker and inform them of the situation. Tell them I'll send copies of the marriage certificate right away." Before Deb could answer, she added, "And would you pack a few of my things and send them to me?"

"Yes, what do you want me to send?"

"I'll make a list and drop it in the mail. Now, I really must go, love, as Babs is holding lunch for us, and this phone call is going to cost the earth."

"But, Sam," Deb protested.

"I'll call you from the ranch in a few days and answer all your questions, but right now I must run, as Morgan is starting to glower at me. Kiss Bryan for me. Bye for now." Sam hung up quickly.

"Neatly done." Morgan's voice came softly. "Was I glowering?"

Sam chose to ignore him as she walked to the door. He didn't move. "Let me pass," she snapped.

"Not just yet, I have something to say."

Sam felt a shiver run down her spine. Gone was all warmth from his voice. It was cold, hard, and it matched his face.

"I've had enough of your sulkiness, Samantha. Now you'll either shake yourself out of it, or I'll do it for you."

"How dare you—" she began, but he cut in roughly, "I dare one hell of a lot and if you want to find out how much, keep pushing. You had your chance to back out and didn't. So put a smile on that beautiful face, for we are leaving this room now and joining our friends for lunch and you'd better behave like the lady you're supposed to be, or believe me you'll wish to heaven you had."

Sam stood stiff with anger a few seconds, but his reference to Babs and Ben had hit home. She was being unfair to them. She thought, with shame, of the uneasy glances both had given her all morning. Turning to him with a half smile she murmured, "You're quite right, shall we declare a temporary truce?"

"No, Samantha," he shook his head firmly. "Not temporary, it will have to be a permanent one. This bargain of ours can't work if we don't."

Lunch went well, Sam not missing the look of relief on Babs's face at her thawed attitude. As Sam kissed and hugged Babs, Ben, and Benjie and said good-bye to Marie and Judy, Morgan stashed their suitcases in the car, promising Babs he'd bring Sam to visit soon. They drove the first twenty miles in silence and Sam jumped when Morgan asked suddenly, "Who's Bryan?"

"What?" Then, remembering her phone call, "Deb's fiancé. Why?"

He shrugged in answer, changing the subject. "Sara will have supper ready for us when we get home."

Home? She was going to a house she'd never seen, with a man she didn't know. Home? Her home was in Long Island. She said none of this out loud. Instead she raised delicate brows. "Sara?"

"Sara Weaver, my housekeeper."

"Oh, yes, Babs mentioned her," Sam murmured. "She knows about us?" He glanced at her quickly and nodded, then turned his eyes back to the road. A good driver herself, Sam had been watching him and decided he drove expertly, his big hands easy on the wheel. But as he also drove very fast, except for a few quick glances shot at her, he kept his eyes on the road.

Suddenly he slowed the car, pulled it off to the side of the road, and brought it to a stop. Sam looked at him, startled. "Something wrong?"

"No." Reaching around to the back seat he produced a Thermos bottle. "Marie supplied us with coffee, we may as well stretch our legs and drink it." Pushing his door open he got out and walked around to her as she slid out her side.

Standing together, he leaning against the car, they drank coffee from plastic cups and he said casually, "You seemed surprised that I'd called Sara." Sam nodded. "I had to give her some warning." At her questioning look he added, "She's house proud, probably been cleaning the place ever since I called her." He laughed ruefully. "If I'd have sprung you on her without giving her time to do her thing, she'd have had my hide nailed to the kitchen door."

"I see," Sam said, then asked hesitantly, "Does she know the circumstances?"

He grinned, his eyes laughing at her. "As to sleeping arrangements?" Sam felt her face grow hot and she looked away from him nodding. The beast was laughing at her, she could hear it in his voice.

"No, I simply told her what room to get ready for you. She didn't like the idea very much." His voice went dry. "I explained that within the social stratum in which you were raised, it is not at all unusual for a husband and wife to have separate rooms. She accepted that grudgingly."

Sam looked up at him in amazement. Accepted grudgingly? An employee?

He read her face and the easy, relaxed look on his own became hard, his voice cold. "Understand this, Samantha, Sara is not the hired help. She's family."

Sam, who had started to relax as they talked, stiffened, not from his words, but his tone.

Misunderstanding her withdrawal, he went on. "If Sara dislikes you, she'll still tolerate you because you're my wife. But if she likes you, she'll probably adopt you and be ordering you around and fussing over you before the weekend's out. Either way you will treat her with respect." Turning, he jerked the door open. "Let's get moving."

She got into the car without looking at him and sat rigid, staring straight ahead. She wanted to explain that she did understand his feelings in regard to Sara, had understood since Babs had told her of it. But his cold face stopped her.

He slid under the wheel, tossed the Thermos onto the backseat and put his hand on the key, but didn't turn it. Swearing softly, he turned angrily and grabbing her shoulders forced her to face him. The hardness vanished from his face when he saw hers. Her eyes held a hurt look and her lips trembled slightly. His eyes hung on her mouth a long moment before glancing up to her own. "I didn't mean to sound harsh, but I had to make it clear that I will not have Sara hurt." His tone had softened. "Do you understand?"

"You love her very much, don't you?" Sam whispered, wondering at the small twinge of pain she felt inside when he answered simply, "Very much." He let go of her suddenly, as if just realizing he was still holding her. "Jacob too." Taking two cigarettes from the pack on the dash he lit one, handed it to her, then lit his own.

"Who's Jacob?"

"Sara's husband." Dragging deeply, he narrowed his eyes against the smoke. "Didn't Babs mention Jake?" At the brief shake of her head, he explained. "When my father and mother got married, Sara stated firmly her Miss Betty was not going to Nevada without her." Sam nodded, indicating she knew this. "At the same time, Jake stated equally firmly that Sara wasn't going without him. They were married three days after my parents."

"What does Jake do?"

"Name it. The place would fall apart without him." He

grinned at her easily, relaxed again. "In fact, if my father had left him in charge when he went traipsing the world, instead of hiring that damned manager, I'd have come home to a much different situation."

His eyes looked back through the years a few seconds, then he gave a short laugh. "Mainly Jake keeps the place in order and takes care of anything that grows." At her raised eyebrows he added, "He was a farmer in the Pennsylvania Dutch country, and I wouldn't be surprised if he could make a fence post grow."

She laughed, the tension gone again. Smiling, he started the engine and pulled the car onto the road. The big car ate up the miles with Morgan's foot on the gas pedal. Sam, growing tired, rested her head back and fell asleep. She woke when the car stopped. Opening her eyes slowly, she asked, "Why are we stopping?"

"We're home."

Sitting up quickly, she looked up to see Morgan watching her, his body slightly turned toward her, his left forearm resting on the steering wheel. She looked around in confusion, not fully awake, and saw they were parked on a drive in front of a garage. The house was to the left of it, a breezeway connecting the two. She opened her door and stepped out awkwardly. Massaging the back of her neck, she looked the place over as Morgan took their valises from the back.

The house was a rancher, built in the shape of an L with a smooth lawn surrounding it. In the distance off to the left, Sam could see the ranch outbuildings and a white-railed corral. A flagstone walk ran from the driveway to the front of the house. Morgan led Sam along it to the front. As they neared the door, it was flung open to reveal a full-bodied woman of medium height with a smile on her plain, unlined face.

"Welcome home, and congratulations, Mr. Morgan." She fairly beamed at him, then turned expectantly to Sam. "Thank you, Sara," Morgan said, turning to Sam. "Samantha this is Sara Weaver—Sara, my wife, Samantha."

Sam put out her hand. "How do you do, Sara?" Sara grasped Sam's fingers in her broad, work-roughened hand. "I'm fine and I hope you'll be happy here, Mrs. Wade."

"Sam," Sam replied automatically. Sara said almost the same as Marie had done just one week ago. "Mrs. Sam."

"All right, Sara," Sam laughed, looking around as they moved into the room.

They were in the living room, and the door they had come through was in the corner of it. The front wall had a large bow window with a deep window seat onto which big, plump gold velvet cushions were tossed. Two comfortable-looking chairs with a low table between them were placed in front of the windows. On the far left wall was an archway leading into a hall and in the far left corner were a long, curved sofa with a long oval coffee table in front of it and a wooden rack holding papers and magazines at each end. On the right wall, Sam had noticed as she entered an archway through which she'd glimpsed the dining area. And in that wall between the archway and the back wall was a large, stone fireplace in front of which was another coffee table and two huge chairs with matching hassocks. The floor was hardwood with furry rugs scattered about, and the walls paneled in dark walnut. The ceiling was opened beamed, the beams darkly gleaming against the flat white plaster between. The room was all in white and gold and shades of brown, none of the pieces matching, all blending, and it was as inviting as a pair of warm arms. But what drew Sam was the back wall, like the one in her room at Babs's—it was entirely glass, with sliding doors which led, as Sam saw as she walked up to them, onto a broad porch with outdoor furniture casually placed. Three steps led off the porch to a flagstone walk set in the lawn which sloped gently fifty feet to a shallow bank with a rock garden. Three stone steps down the bank the lawn leveled off, smooth and flat as a putting green and at the base of it a flagstone patio encircled a kidney-shaped swimming pool, its water now reflecting the last long rays of the late afternoon sun. This was Sam's favorite time of day, when those last golden rays bathed everything in a deep, warm glow, softening even the most harsh of outlines. *How perfect to have my first look at this time,* Sam thought fleetingly, and turned back to the two people who had watched her silently the last few minutes. Her eyes alive with pleasure, she turned to Morgan. "It's beautiful, Morgan."

"Yes," his voice echoed her softness. No stiltedly polite "thank you" or overly casual "glad you like it." Just simply, "yes."

Turning to Sara, her eyes still glowing, Sam sighed, "How I envy you this house."

Sara understood. Sam had acknowledged her place in the house. Sara granted Sam's own with, "I happily give it to you." As had happened so many times before, Sam had entered and conquered. Sara was hers. Morgan stood, a small smile tugging the corner of his mouth, as the bond was forged between the two, so different, women.

"Now come with me, Mrs. Sam," Sara said briskly, moving to the suitcases inside the door. "I'll show you your room. You'll want to wash up, and supper's ready to be served."

Morgan also reached for the suitcases. Sara, snatching Sam's up, scolded, "I'll take that, Mr. Morgan, you get cleaned up yourself, if you want to eat." Sam laughed, as

Sara added, as if to a grubby little boy, "Don't you dare come to the table in those jeans."

The idea of anyone speaking like that to that big, arrogant, black-eyed devil amused Sam greatly and she had trouble controlling her face as Morgan replied dryly, "Samantha's wearing jeans."

"Well, they're different somehow on a lady. Don't you dare, Morgan," Sara tacked on warningly, forgetting the Mister.

Morgan laughed out loud, shaking his head as he watched Sara lead Sam across the room to the arched hallway.

It was a short one, some twelve or fourteen feet, Sam thought, leading into another at a right angle. There was a door on each wall and Sara nodded to the one on their left. "Mr. Morgan's office." Eyeing Sam, she indicated the one on the right. "*His* bedroom."

They turned to the right at the joining and Sam saw a much longer hall, realized this part of the house was the downward stroke of the L. A few steps along the hall and Sara stopped, opened a door on the left, and waited for Sam to enter. Sam's breath caught and she stood quietly a few seconds glancing around. The room was done completely in white and shades of green: the deep-piled carpet in forest, so deep it looked almost black, the walls and ceiling in pale apple, and the draperies at two large windows on the far wall and bedspread in a deep summer leaf green. The woodwork and furniture were in sparkling spotless white. Sam loved it.

"I hope you'll be comfortable here." Sara looked around doubtfully. The idea of a husband and wife not sharing the same room obviously did not sit well with her.

Sam, smiling slightly, murmured, "I don't see how I could help but be, it's a lovely room."

"And here's your bathroom," Sara added, walking across the room to the left. She opened the door to reveal a large bath in deep pink and gold. *It's as if someone knew my colors,* Sam thought.

"Now don't bother unpacking," Sara said, going to the door. "I'll do that later. You wash up and come right in for supper."

Sam smiled as the door closed with a snap, remembering Morgan's warning that if Sara liked her she'd be fussing and ordering her about. Laughing softly, she went into the bathroom. Apparently Sara liked her.

CHAPTER 4

Sam stood staring out through the glass wall, idly smoking a cigarette. The late afternoon sunrays again bouncing and dancing off the pool's water. She didn't really see it, as she was deep in thought. She had been here ten days now, and so far things had gone much more smoothly than she had anticipated. She saw very little of Morgan, as he was gone by the time she got up in the morning and seldom returned to the house before seven. Then he'd come striding through the house to his room to have a quick shower and change in time to sit down to dinner at seven thirty. After dinner he'd sit with Sam in the living room long enough to drink his coffee then, going to the liquor cabinet built into the wall between the dining room archway and the fireplace, he'd drop the inevitable one ice cube in a short, fat glass, splash Jack Daniel's over it, murmur "excuse me" and go into his office. Sam would not see him again except for a quick glance into the office when she said good night on her way to her own room a few hours later.

He had told her the first evening after her arrival that he'd leave the office door open a bit in case she had any questions as to where anything was. Sam had replied lightly, not looking up from her book, "That's quite all right, don't bother, I'll ask Sara if I need anything." She'd looked up in shock when he said quietly, "Sara does not sleep in the house, Samantha. She and Jake have their own small place on the other side of the garage."

"But, I thought—" she began. He cut in, his eyes wicked, the corner of his mouth twitching in amusement. "There's nothing to be afraid of, I'll be here." Laughing softly under his breath, he'd gone to his office.

Sam had not slept well those first few nights, but on finding that once in her room she heard nothing, not even Morgan going to his own room, whatever time that might be, she had shaken off the uneasy feeling and had slept well since.

On her first day at the ranch Morgan had not worked, at least not on the property. He had wakened her early, tapping on her bedroom door insistently until she'd groaned, "Yes, what is it?"

"Roll out, Red," he'd ordered. "My men will be expecting to meet you this morning. You have twenty-five minutes, so you'd better get moving."

Still groaning, Sam had bitten back some very nasty words as she dragged herself off the bed. Twenty minutes later she'd strolled into the kitchen, still half asleep but looking perky in jeans, a heavy knit pullover, and a soft suede jacket.

Morgan's eyes had skimmed over her coolly before shifting to the wall clock. Handing her a cup of coffee, he'd said, "That'll have to do for now. We'll eat later."

Sam had gulped down the hot brew, then followed him through the still, pink dawn to the outbuildings she'd spotted briefly the day before. A small group of men stood, hats in hands, waiting for them. With surprising abruptness Morgan made the introductions, then turned away from her to give the men work instructions.

Feeling dismissed, wondering at the hot shaft of pain the feeling caused, Sam walked to the corral fence, breath catching at the sight that met her eyes. Standing inside the corral, elegant head arched high, bathed in the first sharp rays of morning sun, was the most beautiful golden palomino Sam had ever seen. As if recognizing she had a captive audience, the mare tossed her head and danced delicately to the corral fence, allowing Sam to stroke her long nose.

"She's a beauty, isn't she?"

Not having heard Morgan walk up to her, Sam jumped at his softly drawled voice.

"Yes, she is," Sam sighed, hand dropping to her side.

"She's yours."

With a small gasp, Sam spun around to stare into his strangely watchful face. "But—"

"To ride," Morgan inserted softly. "When I have the time to take you out." Before she could ask him when that would be, he added, as if he had read her thoughts, "After you've become accustomed to the house—and me."

How many times since then had she gone over his words trying to determine exactly what he'd meant? Sam asked herself now. He had not mentioned taking her out again and pride demanded Sam not ask him.

Sam blinked her eyes and saw that the daylight was just about gone. She knew she should go bathe and dress for dinner, but she lit another cigarette and stood still, wondering how Morgan would react to Sara's dinner surprise.

She and Sara had become quick friends, chatting easily and comfortably on any subject that came to hand. Though shocked at the idea when Sam first mentioned it, Sara had given in to Sam's pleading to help with the housework as she found time hanging on her hands. Sara had assigned Sam light duty, as Sam called it, admonishing her sternly not to let Morgan find out about it. Sara considered Sam, to Sam's deep amusement, too much a lady for heavy housework. But two days ago Sam had managed to invade Sara's kitchen.

On Thursday, Jake had carried the large cardboard carton containing the things Sam had asked Deb to pack and send her into Sam's room. Sam had liked Jake at first meeting. Not much taller then his wife, he was broad in the shoulders, strong as an ox and gentle as a kitten. His wife bossed him around outrageously and he loved it, as did his boss.

"Here are your things, Mrs. Sam," he'd called to her through her bedroom door. Sam had flung open the door with an "Oh, thank you, Jake, I imagine you were all getting a trifle tired of seeing me in the same clothes all the time."

"Oh, I don't know about that." He gave her a shy grin. "I think you always look pretty, no matter what you wear," he complimented as he left the room. His tone was that of an affectionate parent. Jake had adopted Sam too.

Sara had come into the room to help Sam unpack the bulging carton. Touching things lovingly, exclaiming in delight, she had put the beautiful clothes, shoes, and handbags in the closet, placed books in the case by the bed and records next to Morgan's in the rack in the TV-stereo unit built into the wall on the other side of the fireplace. Then her eyes lit up when she realized what was in the notebooks at the very bottom of the carton. Sam's recipes were her passport to Sara's kitchen.

They had sat, drinking coffee, at the kitchen table every moment Sara could spare since. Sara studied the recipes, Sam translating the ones in French, and just yesterday had declared she would try one on Morgan, with Sam's help of course. "Do we dare?" Sam had asked impishly.

The meals Sam had eaten since arriving had all been delicious and perfectly prepared, most with a decidedly

German flavor, some strictly American. But due to the wide variety of foods Sam was used to, quite a few of which she had cooked herself in the big kitchen in the house in Long Island, she was well ready for a change.

"Oh, Mr. Morgan's been around," Sara had returned airily. "I wouldn't be surprised to find he'd tasted most of these at one time or other." Sam, considering Morgan's unconcerned attitude to whatever was placed before him at the dinner table, forbore to comment.

They had studied and discussed the different recipes when Sara finally chose a Viennese cream torte. Sam, thinking, they wouldn't have to face the music till the end of the meal.

Now she turned sharply as Morgan strode into the living room. His brows shot up as he glanced at his watch before his eyes skimmed over Sam's jeans and ribbed top. "Aren't you changing for dinner?"

"What time is it?" she asked, her own eyes taking in his stockinged feet, dusty jeans and shirt, and the broad-brimmed Andalusian hat he had brought home from a trip to Spain that he wore low on his forehead. "Seven thirty," he supplied and laughed softly as she cried, "It can't be," making a dash for the hall, his long stride right behind her.

She had a swift shower, hurried into her bikini panties and bra, applied makeup lightly, pulled the pins from her hair, and shook her head to loosen its long coil. She brushed her hair quickly and glancing at the clock, decided there was no time to recoil it. It would have to hang loose. Sliding her feet into gold sandals, she pulled a silky gold and brown caftan from her closet and over her head. She gave her hair a last smoothing with the brush, then, tossing the long, heavy hair back off her shoulders, left the room.

Morgan turned from the liquor cabinet, a drink in each

hand, as Sam entered the living room. He watched her as she walked across the floor to him and she felt her chin lift and her back stiffen as he studied her. His eyes were insolent as they went over her face and hair, his brow inching at the mass of it freed from its usual coil. Slowly his hooded eyes moved down her body and back up again, to linger long seconds on the neckline of her gown where it plunged deeply between her breasts. She felt her face grow warm at his appraisal and in retaliation coolly raked her own eyes down the length of his body. That he looked unnervingly attractive she had to admit to herself. His black hair curled at the nape of his neck, shiny and still damp from the shower. His lean brown face, the cheeks smooth, gleamed with a freshly shaven look. His black brows rose over eyes amused at her survey. His silk shirt was startlingly white against the dark skin of his throat and chocolate brown slacks that fit snugly on his slim hips and down the long legs to flare gently at the bottom. When her eyes lifted to his, his voice held mocking laughter. "Enjoy the view?"

Anger flashed from cold green eyes and she replied icily, "Just another man."

His laughter was derisive, his voice low. "And for five million dollars you expected more, is that it?"

Sam went rigid with fury. Barely able to control her voice, she seethed, "How dare you!"

He answered softly. "I think you'll find out before too long, Samantha, that I dare anything." The amusement had left his voice and his face was deadly serious. Sam felt a small twinge of fear. Before she could answer he put in smoothly, "Shall we have our dinner?" He strolled into the dining room, leaving her to follow him.

She seated herself across from him, refusing to look at him, and forced herself to smile at Sara as she served dinner. The dessert took on more significance as they ate silently, and Sam was sorry she'd ever asked Deb to send her the notebooks. Finally Sara sat the torte in front of him and stepped back, an anxious look on her face, waiting for him to taste it. *Good Lord,* Sam thought, *one would think she was afraid he'd beat her if he didn't like it.*

One eyebrow raised, he looked first at Sara, then at Sam before tasting it. "An excellent torte, Sara," he complimented quietly. "I don't recall you serving this before."

"Thank you, Mr. Morgan." Sara's voice was tinged with pride. "You're right, I haven't made this before. It's one of Mrs. Sam's recipes and she helped me make it."

"No kidding," Morgan answered sardonically. "I hadn't realized Mrs. Sam was so domesticated." He smiled gently at Sara's confused look, which turned to relief at his smile. Smiling happily, she left the room.

Sam glared at him across the table as he calmly ate his dessert. When he had finished, his eyes again slowly raked over her. "My heavens," he mocked, "all this and she cooks too."

They drank their coffee in silence, Sam's eyes smoldering, Morgan's amused. As soon as he put his cup down, he stood up, poured his whiskey, and went to his office. Tonight he did not excuse himself.

Sam carried the coffee tray to the kitchen and complimented a beaming Sara. At her suggestion they try another recipe soon, Sam voiced a vague, "Yes, well, we'll see," and hastily left the room. She went straight to her bedroom, not bothering to say good night to Morgan as she passed the office door. Once inside her room she kicked off her sandals and sat down at her small desk to write to Deb.

She had written four lines in twenty-five minutes when she threw the pen down and stood up. Pacing back and forth in agitation, she thought, *Damn that cowboy for annoying me like this, what is the purpose of it?* She couldn't think of any reason and, giving up, decided to read, hoping that would calm her, and glanced about for her book. Not seeing it, she went back into the living room in search of it and was drawn to the wall of glass by the shimmering glow of moonlight. Standing still, transfixed by the dance the moonlight was doing on the pool's water, she didn't hear Morgan come up behind her. She jumped, then spun around sharply at his softly whispered words. "Still mad, Redhead?"

Her voice was a hiss through her teeth. "I detest being called Red."

He laughed, low in his throat, and caught her off guard saying, "That's a beautiful dress." She was groping for a retort when he bent his head, brushed her lips with his own, as he had done twice before, and whispered. "And you're a beautiful woman." His mouth brushed hers again and, one big hand going around her neck under her hair, the other around her waist, he pulled her to him. His mouth pressed down on hers, his lips forcing her own open. Sam went still in his arms a moment in shock, but his hard, demanding mouth seemed to be robbing her of strength. She couldn't think, felt oddly lightheaded, and without her willing it, her arms slid up around his neck, her body went soft against him. His arms became hard, coiled bands that pulled her tightly against the hard length of him, robbing her of breath.

His mouth left hers, went to the curve of her neck, sending tiny shivers down her spine. The hand at the back of her neck slid to her arm and grasping her firmly drew her back away from him as his lips trailed along the neckline of her gown to stop and caress the soft skin at the V between her breasts. His other hand slid sensuously over her hip.

75

Sam felt like her body had been set on fire. Desperately trying to fight a confusing urge to surrunder, she gasped, "Morgan, you must stop."

Lifting his head, he bent low over her. His lips almost touching hers, he said fiercely, "I must not stop. I want you, Samantha, and I'm going to have you. Now." With those words he clamped his mouth on hers passionately, his lips bruising hers. All resistance went out of her and she clung to him feeling she could no longer stand up. Feeling her go limp against him, Morgan bent and scooped her up. Holding her tightly in his arms he carried her into his bedroom.

Sam lay tightly against Morgan's body, her head resting on his chest. She couldn't move, for although he was asleep, his arm still held her. She had made one tentative attempt to move away once and the arm had tightened. Now she pressed against him almost afraid to breathe. She didn't want to wake him. She wept silently.

He had been an expert lover, if a little rough at first. When she had cried out in pain, he had become very still. His voice an incredulous whisper, he exclaimed. "My God, Samantha, I had no idea!" Her outcry had not stopped him, but he had become gentle, almost tender, his hands, his mouth, caressing, building in her a hunger almost as great as his own. Her cheeks burned now, remembering how she had surrendered, willingly, eagerly, to his possession of her, making her his. But she had been his, she admitted to herself now, the damp, matted hair on his chest soft against her cheek, from the beginning. From the minute she had walked into Babs's living room and had felt the impact of his black eyes on her, she had been his.

She shivered and his arms tightened. She didn't want to

love him. She thought of Ben, tender, affectionate, his eyes warm with love when he looked at Babs. That was the kind of man she had wanted to love. Not this hard, unfeeling, cold-eyed cowboy who laughed at her mockingly. That he wanted her physically, he had just proven. Seemingly tireless, he'd drawn her to him again and again, murmuring softly of a hunger that gnawed, a thirst that raged. In a mindless vortex of pleasure created by his caressing hands, his exciting mouth, Sam had floated in an unbelievably beautiful state of sensual sensation, until sheer exhaustion caught him, sent him into a deep sleep. No, she didn't want to love him, yet she faced the fact she was his. She did love him. She wept silently.

Sam woke slowly and stretched languidly, feeling completely relaxed and free of tension for the first time in weeks. Opening her eyes fully, she stiffened, shame flooding through her as she remembered the night before. She was alone, the house was very quiet, and she knew by the bright sunlight shining through the window that faced the porch, the only window in the room, that it was late in the day. Good Lord! Had she slept most of the day away? She had been exhausted till she had finally slept. The blackness of the room had changed to a pale gray. Now, the room in bright light, she looked around, she had not been in Morgan's bedroom before, not even when Sara had shown her the house. The bed she was lying in was huge, the biggest bed Sam had ever seen in her life, and at this moment was quite rumpled, a fact which made Sam's face warm. The walls and ceiling between the open beams were white, the furniture dark walnut. The carpet and matching draperies Mediterranean blue. Through the open bathroom door she could see that room was in black and white tile, even the towels were black and white. No frills, almost Spartan, definitely a man's room.

She jumped out of bed suddenly, thinking, I've got to get out of here, and her cheeks flamed again. She had not a stitch on. Her caftan and undies lay draped on the white chair in the corner, and she knew Morgan had picked them up, for when he had removed them the night before, they had been dropped carelessly in a heap on the floor.

Snatching them up and holding the gown against herself she opened the bedroom door cautiously, peeking out. Seeing the hall empty she dashed for her own room, sighing with relief as she closed the door behind her.

The salty drops mingled with the water as Sam stood numbly under the jet spray of the shower. She had to go, she decided, and it tore at her heart. Not to be near him, not to see him—the thought was almost unbearable. But she knew she had no choice, for how long would it be, if she stayed, before those mocking black eyes, filled with contempt, told her he knew how she felt?

Sam moved back and forth in the room packing her suitcase. She'd take only what she needed, Sara could send the rest of her things East later. She knew Sara was not in the house now, as she always had Sunday free after preparing the noon meal. And it was now after five. Sam had no idea if Morgan was in the house or not, as she had not left her room after fleeing his.

She went into the bathroom to collect her toiletries and stopped in her tracks as she came back into the bedroom. Morgan was leaning lazily against the bedroom doorframe, his thumbs hooked through two of the belt loops on his close-fitting jeans. The breath caught in Sam's throat. *What a magnificent male animal he is,* she thought. *Like a huge cat, at ease, relaxed, yet giving the impression of being ready to spring in an instant.* She felt a slight shiver as she watched him. His eyes went over her clothes and valise on the bed, the open closet door and bureau drawer. Then his cool glance came to rest on her. His voice was unconcerned.

"Running away, Redhead?"

Sam had control of herself now. She had had her cry, and in a cool, composed voice she answered, "I'm going home."

One black eyebrow arched and he drawled, "Really, I thought you were home." Before she could say anything he went on, "How are you going to explain your sudden appearance alone? Don't you think it will sound a little strange if, after assuring them you were in love, you tell them that after two weeks of marriage your husband raped you?"

Without stopping to think Sam gasped, "But you didn't," then stopped, shocked at her own denial.

Morgan laughed softly. "I know, I just wanted to make sure you did."

"I won't stay here," Sam snapped angrily.

"Why not?" Black eyes went over her slowly and Sam felt herself grow warm. She had not dressed after showering, but had slipped on a terry robe, belting it tightly. She moved away from his look, her bare feet silent on the carpet as she went to place her makeup bag in the suitcase. "You know why," she flung over her shoulder.

"Yes," he answered dryly. "Because you thought you'd bought yourself a man's name, and now you find the man came with it."

"How dare you," she breathed indignantly. "We made an agreement, a marriage in name only."

"I warned you last night, Redhead, I dare almost anything."

"I told you not to call me that," Sam said hotly, but he went on as if he hadn't heard her. "And I made no such agreement, not when Ben first talked to me about it or when you and I discussed it later. If there were terms and conditions, it seems you forgot to tell me at the time, and it's a little late now." He paused, then added gently, "I'm sorry if I hurt you last night, but I had no way of knowing of your—er—virginal state."

"What kind of girl did you think I was?" Sam cried.

"I thought you were a woman," he snapped sharply. "My God, Samantha, you're going to be twenty-five soon. I didn't think any young woman reached that age and remained innocent today and I'll call you Redhead or anything else I damn well please."

Sam's cheeks were hot, and she opened her mouth to protest, but he hadn't finished. "I said I'm sorry I hurt you and I mean that, but I'm glad I was the first." Sam lowered her eyes so he could not read them as she thought, *I'm glad too.* Turning from him, she walked to the closet and reached blindly toward her clothes. Her hand stopped, became still, as his voice, hard now, lashed at her. "So you're going to run, throw it all away, because you haven't the guts to grow up."

Sam spun around, glaring at him. "What do you mean, throw it all away?"

Morgan's eyes were as cold as his voice. "I mean there'll be no polite little visits every now and then, so you don't lose the money. I'll divorce you, Samantha, and you can live off your stepmother until you find a man who'll marry you under your conditions. Or you might fall in love, if you're capable, and the physical side of it won't be so abhorrent to you."

"You really are a beast," she whispered.

"Maybe so," he said, his voice flat. "But that's beside the point. It's up to you. You can go or stay. But make no mistake, if you stay, what happened last night will happen again regularly." His voice hardened. "You can hate my guts for the next five years, but you'll stay put, I'll see to that. There will be no little side trips alone. If you want to go anywhere, it will be with me. And don't think I can't keep you here—I can." At the look which had come into her face as he spoke, he sighed in exasperation, rasped, "What the hell did you expect, Samantha? Did you really think we could live in the same house for five years without sex? Or did you suppose I'd keep a girl friend somewhere and drive back and forth after working fourteen hours a day?" She opened her mouth to answer him, but he went on harshly. "If you go now, it will be final. So make up your mind. What's it going to be, go or stay?"

Sam's eyes were wide, unbelieving. "You want an answer now? This minute? You won't give me time to think about it?"

He had moved into the room as he talked and now he stood, not more then two feet in front of her. His face was expressionless, his voice rough. "I've given you two weeks to think. As a matter of fact you should have thought it out before you married me. If you'll remember, I asked you if you had second thoughts the night before we got married. You assured me then that you didn't. You've had more than enough time, Samantha. What's it going to be?"

Sam turned away so he couldn't see her face. *He means it,* she thought wildly, *he'll divorce me. I won't see him again.* He had said, not knowing how she felt, she might fall in love. But she knew, somehow, deep inside, there would never be another man for her. It would be hell, she knew, if she stayed. Not being able to show her love, having him use her body to relieve his physical needs. But it would be worse not to be near him, not to see him at all. In a small, tired whisper she said, "I'll stay." Without a word, he turned her around and pulled her into his arms.

CHAPTER 5

Spring fever, lovesickness, Sam had both, and though she readily gave in to one, she silently riled at the other. What had she ever done to deserve Morgan Wade? The mere thought of his name set off a tingling reaction throughout her system that left her weak, longing for the sight of him.

From the time she was fourteen, Sam had been besieged by admirers. Some coaxed, some pleaded, a few even begged for a chance to make her care for them, but Sam had blithely gone her way, untouched, unmarked by any of them. The idea that, of all the men she'd known, this lean, long-legged cowboy could ignite her senses to the point of near madness, was a very bitter pill to swallow. For Morgan didn't coax, and Morgan didn't plead, and most emphatically, Morgan didn't beg. Morgan demanded. The fact that she gave in without demurs to his demands was the confidence-shattering self-knowledge that Sam riled against.

Sam slowed the mare to a walk and drank in the sweetness of spring on the land. *Being the complete idiot I am,* she thought wryly, a small smile of self-mockery twisting her lips, *I not only allow myself to become enslaved to the man, I go off the deep end for his land as well.* Bringing the horse to a complete stop, Sam idly stroked the mare's beautifully arched, golden neck, her eyes pinpointing the ranch buildings. When he had had the palomino cut out of the corral for her, Morgan had warned her not to lose sight of the buildings when she rode alone. Green eyes flashing rebelliously, Sam had turned on him angrily, but he cut off her hot protest before she could voice it.

"I mean it, Samantha. I don't want you riding out alone. I don't have the time, nor can I spare the men, to launch a search for you if you get lost. Which you probably would." Morgan paused, black eyes hard with determination. Then, seeing the disappointment she couldn't hide on her face, his voice gentled. "I'll take you out when I get the time." A teasing light entered his eyes. "If you're a good girl, Redhead, maybe we'll ride out on Sunday."

They had, and from that first ride across his property, Sam was a goner. Morgan's manner, though teasing, was easy, relaxed, as he showed her the land he so obviously loved. The mountains, with their color shadings at different times of the day, the Indian paintbrush, larkspur, and other spring flowers all had their effect on her. Whether it was the countryside or her guide, Sam wasn't quite sure, but for the first time in her life she felt as if she were home.

As spring faded into summer, and that too wore on, Morgan seemed to work even harder. He looked tired. The smooth skin over his cheeks and jaw grew tight and drawn and his hard slim body became even harder. When he held her at night the muscles in his arms, shoulders, and thighs felt like corded steel. He was drawn to a fine, tough edge and he frightened her a little at times.

Over coffee one evening in late spring Morgan casually told Sam he was thinking of buying a plane, a Lear jet, and just as casually asked her what she thought of the idea. Surprised, and flustered that he'd even bother to ask her, Sam had told him stiffly to do what he thought best, then watched in dismay as his eyes went flat and expressionless.

With a sharp nod of his head he'd left the room, murmuring cryptically, "I always do."

He'd bought the Lear and Sam hoped the plane, enabling him to get around faster, would give him more time. It hadn't. If anything, he seemed to have less.

Unsure of her position in their strange relationship, Sam asked few questions and Morgan volunteered little information. But she did learn, from the few things he did say, and the off-chance remarks made by Sara and Jake, that his interests did not lay wholly in the ranch as she had thought. He was in partnership in ranches in South America and Australia, owned interests in mines in Nevada and Africa, and was involved in other ventures in the States and Europe. She saw little more of him now than she had in the first two weeks of their marriage. He spent most of his time, the evenings he was at home, in his office, usually on the phone. If she had thought at first he had married her with the idea of her money making his life easier, she knew now how wrong she'd been. She had never known a man who worked harder. She felt a deepening respect for him, and she loved him to the point of distraction.

Most nights, when he was home, they slept together. He coming to her room when he'd finished in his office, usually very late. Other than the first time, she had spent only one night in the huge bed in his room.

It had been a particularly lovely night in late spring and Sam, curled into one of the big chairs in the living room, was reading. Morgan had been in his office not much more than an hour when he sauntered into the room and up to her chair. Bending over, he plucked the book from her fingers and as he dropped it to the floor, his voice was low, almost raw.

"It's too nice a night to waste, Redhead."

Scooping her into his arms, he'd carried her to his bedroom. Sam liked it there in that big bed. For some strange reason she felt more his wife in his bed. He had not taken her there again.

Her tears still wet his chest before she slept, but no longer from a feeling of shame. She honestly admitted to herself that her own physical need of him matched his for her. She wept now from frustration and fear. Frustration at having to wear a mask, hiding her true feelings from him. Fear that his own seemingly insatiable appetite for her would slacken and she'd find herself alone at night as well as in the daylight.

She was alone too much and now, in early August, it was beginning to show. She was losing weight. She ate very little when Morgan was home and hardly anything when he wasn't. Sara fussed over her to no avail. She simply was not hungry. Not for food.

Time was heavy, the days too long. The small jobs Sam found to do, the light housework, a small amount of cooking, puttering in the small garden Jake had helped her lay out, did not take nearly enough time. She went riding, but though she had always before enjoyed riding alone, it had somehow lost all appeal. She swam and sunbathed, her normal light tan turning to a deep golden color. She read. She paced. She wanted to scream. She grew tense and strained and was consumed with jealousy. Morgan was away often. He'd tell her casually the night before he left that he'd be away a few days. A few days often stretched into a week. She was positive there was another woman, possibly more than one. She knew that with a man like Morgan, handsome, charming when he chose to be, with a look of complete sensual masculinity, the women would gravitate to him, unable to keep their eyes or hands off him. When he was away, she hated him fiercely.

Sam had been away from the ranch only twice in the almost four and a half months she'd lived there. And for a young woman who was used to tearing around the world at the merest suggestion, the confinement was not easy to live with.

On a Friday evening not long after he had bought the jet, Morgan told Sam he had to fly to San Francisco in the morning. That statement alone surprised her as he never bothered to tell her where he was going, just that he was. After a small pause her surprise changed to an almost childlike excitement when he asked her if she'd care to go with him, adding that she could do some shopping while he took care of his business and then they could have dinner, perhaps see a show, and fly home Sunday morning. Sam forced her voice to sound calm, not wanting to appear overeager, and said she'd enjoy that, as she did have some shopping she could do. At the odd look that flashed quickly across his face, she had wondered miserably if he'd hoped she'd refuse. Nevertheless she had enjoyed the trip. Morgan was relaxed, charmingly attentive, which Sam attributed to their being in public, and seemingly quite willing to take Sam anywhere she wished to go.

Sam had shopped for hours but bought only a few things. A pair of riding gloves, two silk shirts, and a pair of terribly expensive white jeans that she couldn't resist, even though, when she'd pulled them on in the fitting room, they fit as though they'd been painted on her. She'd been completely happy with her day and was amused, on entering the hotel room to find Morgan already there, one brow raised at her few packages.

"It took you this long to buy that?"

She hadn't offered to show him what she'd bought, sure he wasn't in the least interested, and after a few long seconds he'd shrugged, dropped onto the bed, said he was going to grab a nap before dinner, and fell promptly asleep.

Their dinner on the Wharf had been superb, the show excellent, and on returning to their hotel room, Morgan's lovemaking ardent. Sam had returned to the ranch content. Her contentment didn't last long, however, as Morgan was away most of the time the next few weeks.

At the beginning of June, when Morgan was again away, and Sam was in what she'd always thought of as her bad time of the month, she thought that although she loved it, if she didn't get away from the house she'd go mad. On the spur of the moment she decided to visit Babs for a few days. Although they talked often on the phone, Sam had not seen Babs since her wedding day. She knew the silver gray Jaguar that Morgan had bought, again consulting her first, was in the garage. She had heard Morgan ask Jake the night before if he'd drive him to the small airfield where he kept the plane, as he wanted to go over some papers on the way, and she'd heard Jake put the car in the garage when he'd returned.

Hurrying into the kitchen, she told a startled Sara to go home and take care of Jake as she was going away for a few days, then had left the room on the fly before Sara could question her. She had thrown some clothes into her suitcase and left before she could change her mind. She was not concerned about driving the Jaguar—she had driven powerful cars ever since she became old enough to drive. What did nag at her was Morgan's words the day he'd given her the choice of go or stay. "If you go anywhere it will be with me." With a snort of impatience at herself, she shook off the feeling of unease and decided firmly she would enjoy herself. She had, although the warm, family atmosphere in Babs's home left her with a lonely, hurt, ache inside.

Morgan came home the day after Sam did. Waiting, like a coward she thought, for the right ti : e to tell him where she'd been, he caught her off guard, as glancing up at her across the dinner table he said softly, "Have a nice vacation, Samantha?" Unable to believe that either Sara or Jake had said anything to him, Sam stammered, surprised, "H-how did you—?"

"You really should have filled the tank, you know," he cut in, his voice like silk. "That Jag eats up the gas." His voice rapped, "Where did you go?"

"To see Babs," she'd snapped, resenting his tone. "We all missed you," she added sweetly, then wished she hadn't, as she saw his eyes narrow.

He stared at her silently a few moments, his eyes glinting warningly. When he spoke, his voice was a threat.

"Next time you want to see Babs, tell me, and if I can take time off we'll go together, or invite them here. Don't go off by yourself again." At the flash of defiance in Sam's eyes he added, much too softly, "I mean it, Samantha."

The spark of fight went out of Sam, and she looked away from him. Why? Oh, why, she thought in self-disgust, did she allow this man to intimidate her like this? She had never in her life retreated from a man before. She didn't like the feeling.

That had been over two months ago, and although Morgan had not gone away as often in the last few weeks, Sam saw very little of him. They ate dinner later, as he stayed out as long as the light held, coming in dusty, his shirt sticking to him in dark wet patches. He slid into Sam's bed earlier than before too, sometimes, but not often, not even making love to her, just taking her into his arms and falling into a deep sleep within minutes.

Sam worked in the morning sun, fitfully pulling weeds in the herb garden behind the kitchen. Morgan had gone away two days before, the first time in weeks, and Sam was feeling moody and as surly as the weather. It had become mucky and close the day before, storms threatening which so far had not materialized, and Sam was hot and sticky and lonely.

She jumped up, pulling the gloves from her hands, on hearing the roar of the Jag as Morgan pulled into the drive. She was around the house and halfway to the car before he cut the engine.

She made herself slow down as she walked to the car, watching him hungrily as he unfolded himself from the driver's seat, then reach back inside for his suitcase. As he turned to her, she felt a stab of pure jealousy, positive he had been with another woman. The lines of strain were gone from his face and he looked rested for the first time in weeks.

He grinned at her, and she almost believed he was glad to see her. "This weather's a bitch isn't it?" Arching a brow at her sweat-soaked shirt and grubby knees below her shorts he added, "What in hell are you doing working in this heat, you crazy redhead? Why aren't you in the pool?"

Sam frowned at the word *redhead*, though she felt an icicle thrill go down her spine. She would never admit it, but she loved the sound of it on his lips. It had become, for her, a substitute for the endearments she never heard.

"You work in the heat." She kept her voice as light as his, not wanting to sour his good mood.

He laughed softly and dropped an arm over her shoulder as they walked toward the kitchen door.

"I wouldn't if I didn't have to," he lied.

The look Sam shot at him called him a liar and he laughed again softly, easily, and the stab of jealousy tore deeply into her. What was she like? Sam tormented herself with the thought. This woman who could make Morgan look and act like this.

He lifted his arm from her shoulder and opened the kitchen door for her to proceed him into the house. Inside he stood still for a second, looking around the empty, silent room. Then he turned sharply to Sam and her heart sank. His face had gone stiff, his eyes hard, and his soft, laughing voice of a moment ago now had a raw edge.

"Where's Sara?"

"She went into town with Jake to do some shopping," Sam answered as lightly as she could.

"You're alone here?" The edge was sharper.

Sam turned away biting her lip. *You don't have to worry, I won't run away,* she wanted to snap, but what she said was, "I don't mind, I like being alone."

"I know." His voice had an odd inflection that Sam couldn't understand. "And what about lunch?"

"Morgan, I am completely capable of preparing my own lunch, for heaven's sake." Sam felt let down and exasperated and now her own voice had an edge.

"I'm aware of that fact."

For some reason Sam didn't understand, his manner had changed again, he was relaxed, his voice light and teasing. "What I'm wondering is, are you prepared to make mine as well?"

"Well, of course!" The face she turned to him wore a surprised look at the abrupt change in him. Would she ever understand this man? Glancing at the clock and noting it was only ten thirty she asked, "Are you hungry? Do you want lunch now?"

"No, I'm not hungry—for lunch." Then he surprised Sam even more by adding, "Suppose you give me a half hour or so to check any messages Sara left on my desk

91

while I've been away, and then we'll have a swim together before we have lunch."

Sam's face looked even more surprised. He'd said it casually, as if they swam together regularly, when in fact they had never shared the pool. She answered quickly, forcing her voice to stay light, "All right, I'll have a shower while you're in your office." And she walked ahead of him out of the kitchen.

Standing under the shower, Sam felt the curl of excitement that had started with Morgan's words building inside. *Don't be a silly child,* she told herself softly, but she couldn't stop the feeling of happiness that washed over her. She felt almost grateful to that unknown woman who had sent Morgan home in such a relaxed mood. She had stepped out of the shower and was wrapping a towel around herself as she thought this and she became perfectly still. *I must surely be going mad,* she thought now, the feeling of happiness dying. The idea that she was thankful to another woman for any small crumb of pleasure Morgan might offhandedly offer her made Sam feel sick. A picture of herself six months ago flashed through her mind. Samantha Denning, laughingly turning her lips away from the mouths of the men she'd gone out with, coolly turning down their offers of marriage, frigidly telling them to keep their hands to themselves when they had reached out to touch her. And now, Samantha Wade, who trembled in the arms of this tall hard-eyed man, whose own arms slid around his neck eagerly as her mouth hungrily accepted his. *Oh, God!* she thought now. *Why should love be like this?* And she felt, for the first time, a measure of compassion for the men who had pleaded with her to marry them.

She stood there quite still, dripping on the bathmat for

a long time, and was jerked into movement by a short rap on her bedroom door as Morgan called.

"Hurry up, Redhead, I'll see you in the pool."

Sam quickly blotted herself off and twisted her hair back as she walked into the bedroom. Taking a long barrette from her dresser, she fastened the silky red mass to the back of her head, then stepped into the bottom of her bikini and gave a sign of dismay, for it hung on her hips. Shaking her head slightly, she reknotted the material, taking in the slack and put on the skimpy top, noting she had to tie that more tightly than before also. She turned to the full-length mirror on the closet door and gave herself a long, critical look. She was not happy with what she saw. She was much thinner, her collarbone and pelvic bones sticking out prominently. She had a dark, bruised look under her eyes and her face had a drawn, strained look. She grimaced in distaste, then turned sharply away, not wanting to look on the pitiful woman reflected there.

Sam stood at the side of the pool, watching Morgan's sinewy, powerful arms slice through the water. As he reached the far end and turned, he saw her and shot back across the pool. Placing his hand on the edge he lifted himself smoothly from the water. He stood in front of her, legs slightly apart, and brushed the shining black hair from his face. Standing still, his eyes raked over her. His voice soft, almost silky, chided, "You look like hell, Redhead, how much weight have you lost?" Reaching out his hand, he trailed his forefinger along her collarbone. "Haven't you been feeling well?" His voice sharpened as his hand moved to grasp her shoulder. "You're not pregnant, are you?"

Sam winced as his fingers dug into her soft flesh. "Of course not," she gasped, wondering at the strange look that sped across his face. "And I'm perfectly well, I've just

93

been minding the heat, I guess." Wanting to change the subject she added quickly, "Doesn't it ever rain here?" It worked, for he laughed, then drawled, "Not much." Looking up at the black clouds moving in the distance he added, "Even though it looks like it might before too long. So let's get our swim while we can." With those words he grabbed her hand and grinned at her squeal as he leaped into the water pulling her with him.

They swam side by side for some time, he matching his strokes to her shorter ones. When she stopped to catch her breath, he slid his big hand around her neck and drew her to him. His mouth close to hers, he whispered, "Let's get out of here, Redhead, I'm hungry." He laughed softly as she gasped and pulled away from him muttering, "Oh! Men!"

Sam stood in her room patting herself dry with the huge towel draped around her and turned swiftly on hearing her door open. Morgan sauntered into the room and Sam turned her back to him feeling her face flush as she clutched the towel firmly to herself. He was wearing nothing but a towel draped loosely about his lean hips and she went tense and rigid as he came up behind her, his arm coiling around her waist. Sliding under the edge of the towel and moving it aside, his hand caressed the smooth, still damp skin underneath. As she felt him lower his head, slide his lips along the sensitive skin on the side of her neck, Sam said breathlessly, "I thought you were hungry?"

His mouth close to her ear, he murmured in amusement, "Yes, but I didn't say what I was hungry for, Redhead." Giving her towel a quick hard tug he dropped it onto the floor as he turned her around into his arms.

"There are those who eat," he purred, "and those who eat."

Her body stiff, Sam decided firmly that this time she would not respond, but her decision wavered when his mouth found hers, his lips hard, demanding, urgent. In the next instant, as she felt his tongue search for and find her own, she sighed and went soft against him, her arms going around his neck, her fingers digging into his hair. He drank even more deeply of her mouth and his arms tightened, the one dropping to her hips, flattening her body against the length of his, letting her know his need of her.

Later, much later, Sam stood at the stove in her robe, watching the eggs she had just poured into the pan. Morgan sat stretched out on a kitchen chair, looking relaxed and somewhat smug. She could feel his eyes on her back, and she jumped at the sound of his voice, low and deep.

"One of the messages on my desk was to call the lawyers Baker."

Sam spun around, her brows raised in question.

"Don't scorch our lunch, kid."

"But what did—?"

"It will wait until we eat," he interrupted.

Sam turned the omelet onto a plate and sat it on the table next to the molded salad she had made early that morning. Seating herself, she turned to Morgan questioning, "What did the Bakers want?"

"Mmm, you really are a terrific cook, Redhead." He put another forkful of eggs into his mouth.

"Morgan." Her voice was low, tinged with warning.

His eyes stared blandly into hers as he slowly chewed and swallowed, the corner of his mouth twitching in amusement as he watched the green eyes start to spark with anger. Just as she was about to explode, he said calmly, "It seems there's a question concerning our finances and they'd appreciate my going to New York to straighten out the problems."

"Are you going?" she asked softly, hesitatingly.

"I suppose I might as well, as Mr. Baker strikes me as the type who would just keep calling until I did," he answered offhandedly.

Sam nodded slowly, pushing the food around on her plate disinterestedly. *He'd said I, not we, but I.* She looked down at her plate and asked softly, a little fearfully, "May I go East with you, Morgan?"

He looked at her silently a few minutes, then his voice mocked. "Have you been a good girl, Samantha?" His eyes gleamed with deviltry as he watched her jerk upright in her chair.

Green eyes blazing, she sputtered, "Really Morgan, I'm not a child, I'll be twenty-five in a few days and you have no right to speak like—"

He cut in sharply, "Calm down, Redhead, and eat your lunch, you're thin enough." He paused, then went on, "That's right, you'll be celebrating a quarter century in a few days." He laughed at the look she threw him. "Now be nice, kid, and I'll think about it while you get my dessert. You do have dessert for me?"

Sam nodded, afraid if she opened her mouth she'd scream at him. She went to the refrigerator and removed the rich creamy rice pudding Sara had made the day before. She served him, then sat stiffly in her chair, poking at the jelled salad in front of her.

"Eat your salad," he ordered, then continued, "The pudding's very good. Aren't you having any?"

She shook her head, her lips tightly compressed. He was deliberately tormenting her, she knew, but she refused to give him the satisfaction of answering him back. Morgan finished his pudding and wiped his mouth with his napkin.

As he tossed it onto the table he said seriously, his face expressionless, "I'll make a bargain with you, Samantha."

Sam looked at him, not answering at once. What was he up to now? she wondered. "What sort of bargain?" she asked finally.

"I'll take you East with me, even stay a week or so in Long Island for you to spend your birthday with your family." Sam caught her breath, but he was going on. "On two conditions."

"What conditions?" Sam breathed, almost afraid to ask.

His eyes held hers, his voice was completely without emotion. "One, tomorrow morning you move your things into my room and, as of tonight, you sleep in my bed. I'm pretty damned tired of crawling out of your bed and trotting to my room to dress every morning." Sam felt her face flame, but his eyes held hers, which widened as he added. "Two, there'll be no more tears, late in the night, every time I make love to you."

So he hadn't been asleep as she'd thought. She hesitated a second and he said impatiently, "Well, will you bargain?" She managed to break the hold of his eyes and lowering hers, she whispered, "Yes."

He pushed his chair back, stood up, and walked around the table to her. Taking her by the shoulders, he lifted her from her chair. He bent his head, kissed her hard, then, lifting his mouth from hers, said softly, "It's a bargain sealed. Can you be ready to go by the end of the week?" Again she whispered, "Yes." Nodding almost curtly he removed his hands and left the room.

CHAPTER 6

Sam rested her head against the seat of the rented Ford and sighed in relief. She had forgotten what New York in August was like.

"Tired?" Morgan glanced at her, then returned his eyes to the highway.

"Not really," Sam settled more comfortably on the seat. "The air-conditioning feels lovely after the heat outside the airport."

He nodded, not looking at her, his eyes steady on the highway, a driver's nightmare with its usual Monday morning traffic heading into New York. Sam lowered her eyelids and looked at him through her lashes, studying him a moment. With his weight loss over the summer the sharply defined lines of his profile were intensified. The skin stretched firm and smooth over the high cheekbones and strong, hard jaw. The color of his skin exposed on his face, throat, and hands had deepened to a rich copper. Sam felt her face grow warm, remembering that except for a lighter swath around his hips, the rest of his body was the same dark color. And she wondered, a little uneasily, when and where he had acquired that color on his long straight legs. The more pronounced leanness had not detracted from his looks. If anything, he was more handsome than when she had first met him.

Morgan felt her eyes and, as one brow inched slowly upward, he drawled, "Something?"

Sam cast about in her mind in confusion and grabbed at the first thing that entered her head. "I—I was just wondering what everyone will think of you." She called herself all kinds of an idiot as she watched the corner of his finely defined lips twitch in amusement.

"I've been meaning to talk to you about that, Redhead." The soft drawl heavier, he added, "I suppose, when we get to Long Island, like it or not, we'll have to play the role of newlyweds."

"Yes, I know." Sam wondered how she had managed to keep her voice so cool. His choice of words had hurt, even though she felt relief wash over her at them. She had become more tense and nervous about this every day since she had agreed to his bargain six days ago. The added days had not helped. Morgan had not been able to get away at the end of the week as he'd planned and had told Sam the trip East would have to wait.

Sam turned her head away from him and closed her eyes, letting her mind drift back over the last six days. She had kept her part of the bargain, and as the threatened storm had finally broken that night, was glad to huddle close to Morgan in the big bed. She had never been afraid of storms, but somehow out there in the space between the mountains, it had seemed so much more threatening. The thunder had rumbled angrily, the lightning cracked long and sharp, brightening the bedroom with its fierce but cold light. Sam had clung to Morgan, feeling safe in his strong, hard arms and ignored the silent laughter that shook his broad chest.

The first few days had not been too bad. She and Sara had been busy, first with transferring Sam's things into Morgan's room, Sara's face telling Sam plainly she thought the move right and proper, then straightening the now empty room. After Thursday night, when Morgan informed her they could not leave until Monday, the tension started to build inside her. She had called Mary and Deb to tell them they were coming, then had had to call them back telling them of the change in plans. She had become steadily more tense, afraid that for some reason or other they would not be able to leave, and if they did, what would be the reaction of her friends and family to Morgan. Then this morning, before daylight, she had awakened to Morgan calling her name softly and had opened her eyes to find his face close to hers as he whispered, "If you're going with me, Redhead, you'd better get moving. I'm leaving in one hour." She'd jumped from the bed and ran to the bathroom, his laughter following her. The flight East had been smooth and uneventful. Morgan flew the jet exactly as he drove the car, expertly.

Sam, bringing her thoughts to the present, opened her eyes and felt a thrill of excitement seeing they were close to the city. Morgan had an appointment with the Messrs. Baker which, Sam noted glancing at her watch, he would make just in time. She planned to do some shopping, her weight loss being such that few of her clothes fit properly. Sam decided she'd look for a special dress, as Mary was planning a belated wedding party and birthday celebration for Friday evening. The thought caused her pain. This was her twenty-fifth birthday. Morgan had forgotten. She gave herself a mental shake, whyever did she think he'd remember.

They reached their hotel and dispensed with the rented car. In the large room Morgan asked if she needed money, which she didn't, told her he had to go or he'd be late, said he'd see her whenever, and left.

Sam went into the bathroom to freshen up and looked

at herself in the mirror. She didn't like what she saw. Her hair pulled back into the usual coil around her head made her face look even thinner than it was. Something had to be done, she decided. She walked quickly to the phone and called her hairdresser. She knew the shop was always closed on Mondays. She also knew he was usually in the shop on Mondays, and was not surprised when she heard his smooth, clear voice answer, something he never did when the shop was open, as he paid a receptionist a very high salary to do it for him.

"Charles?" Sam said, not waiting for a reply as she knew it was him, "Samantha Wa—Denning."

"Samantha," Charles purred. "Wherever have you been, darling? I haven't seen you in ages."

"I've been away, getting married." She answered evenly, and smiled at his reaction.

"What in the world did you want to do that for? Oh, well, no matter, what can I do for you, sweetheart?"

Sam smiled again at the way the endearments rolled off his glib tongue. She knew that many people had doubts about Charles's masculinity, but she had none. If she had ever had any, they had been dispelled the day she found herself alone, not by accident she was now sure, with him in the shop and he'd tried to seduce her in the beautician's chair. She'd had a fight on her hands that day, but she'd won it. He had accepted his defeat graciously, and they were good friends.

"My hair's a sight," she laughed, "and there's a big to-do the end of the week." Sam inserted a pleading note, "Charles, you must help me."

She heard him chuckle softly. "You know I'm closed Monday, you beautiful baggage, but come around and I'll see what I can do with that red mop."

"Thank you, Charles, you're a love." Sam heard him

chuckle again as she replaced the receiver. Six hours later Sam stepped into the hotel elevator and pushed the button for their floor. She felt tired but good, and although she carried only one package, she had spent a lot of money, having all but one outfit sent to the address on Long Island. She smiled to herself as her hand went up to her hair, the long slim fingers sliding into the loose curls. She loved the cut Charles had given her. He had called it a savage cut, short and loosely curled at the top and temples, the crown and sides tapered in length to blend into the long deep waves that fell halfway down her back, which he hadn't touched. She laughed aloud, softly remembering his words as he'd stood back to look at her and admire his own work. "Lord, Sam, you're a beautiful creature. That cut gives you a wild, free look. Why did you do an idiotic thing like get married?"

Her face sobered, *Wild and free.* Well, she certainly hadn't been too wild lately, and she'd never be free again.

She walked into the room and stopped, closing the door softly behind her. Morgan sat sprawled lazily in the chair by the window, reading the *Times,* his long legs stretched out in front of him. He looked up as she entered and went dead still, the paper held motionless. She endured his scrutiny as long as she could. Somehow she managed to keep her voice cool. "Do you like it?"

He folded the paper and dropped it on the floor, his eyes on her, before answering, his voice deep. "You look like a redheaded witch. Are you?" Before she could say anything, he added, "You must be. Cast a spell too. I can feel it doing strange things to me already." His voice went lower. "Come here, Samantha."

"Morgan, I'm hot and tired, I—"

Even lower. "Come here."

"I'm starving, I want my din—"

102

Almost a whisper now, and a definite warning. "Samantha."

Sam walked across the room slowly, dropping the package and her handbag on the bed as she passed. She stopped in front of him and as his hand went to her waist she saw something flash in the late afternoon sunlight coming through the window. His hand drew her down to her knees on the floor between his legs then, taking her left hand, he removed a ring from the end of his finger and slid it along hers till it touched the narrow band of platinum already there. Her eyes widening as she stared at it, she exclaimed. "That's the most beautiful thing I've ever seen!"

The large emerald-cut emerald, set in platinum with two diamond baguettes on either side looked almost too heavy for her slim hand. The deep, clear color of the stone matched the eyes she lifted to his. "Morgan, what—?"

"Happy Birthday, redheaded witch," he murmured.

"I—I don't know what to say," Sam stammered.

He leaned back in the chair, his hands, clasped on her waist, drew her up to him, against him. His mouth an inch from hers, he whispered, "We'll think of some way for you to thank me."

"Are you hungry?" The words were spoken softly when Sam opened her eyes. She turned her head to see Morgan, fully dressed, sitting in the chair by the window.

"Famished," she murmured, her voice blurred with sleepiness. She closed her eyes again. She felt absolutely hollow. She had been looking forward to dinner with longing as she returned from shopping yesterday, and she hadn't had any. Morgan had said he'd think of some way for her to thank him, then had proceeded to show her exactly where his thinking led. As on the first night, he'd been tireless, and she had wondered at the almost desperate urgency of his lovemaking. When, finally, he'd stretched out on his back and drew her into his arms, pulling the covers over them both, she was exhausted, all thoughts of food gone.

"What time is it?" She yawned. Her eyes flew open as he drawled, a hint of laughter in his voice, "Nine thirty."

"Nine thirty! Why didn't you wake me? Dave will be here with the car at eleven." She sat bolt upright, then blushing, clutched the sheet around her nakedness. Morgan laughed out loud and she sat glaring at him. He returned her stare, the corners of his mouth twitching. Sam could see he had no intention of either turning around or leaving the room and her voice became a plea, "Morgan, please."

He shook his head and grinned at her. "You have one hour and thirty minutes to get yourself dressed, fed, and ready to leave this hotel by the time the car gets here. But first, you must get from that bed to that bathroom and I'm quite comfortable where I am, thank you." His grin widened as eyes flashing, she snapped, "Damn you," lifted her chin, threw back the sheet, jumped from the bed and ran for the bathroom.

They walked through the hotel doors just as the midnight-blue Cadillac slid alongside the curb. Dave jumped out to open the door to the back seat, his eyes going over Sam anxiously before, growing guarded, he turned to Morgan.

Sam hurried across the pavement, looking cool and lovely in the pale pink shift and matching sandals she had brought the day before. Stretching out her hand to him she said softly, "Hello, Dave, how are you?"

"I'm fine." He clasped her slim hand firmly a moment, his eyes warm. "Welcome home, Miss Sam."

Morgan stood tall and quiet behind her and, a little breathless, she introduced them. "Dave, this is my husband, Morgan Wade." Turning her head slightly to Morgan, she smiled coolly, and added without a catch, "Darling, our driver and friend, Dave Zimmer."

Morgan was silent, his face expressionless. In confusion Sam turned back to see Dave's eyes study Morgan briefly before extending his hand, Morgan's arm shot past her and as his hand clasped Dave's he said, a small smile twitching his lips, "I assure you, Dave, I'm taking very good care of her."

"Yes, sir, Mr. Wade."

They settled themselves on the back seat and Dave's face, as he slid behind the wheel, told Sam he was satisfied. With a few quiet words, Morgan had acquired a follower.

Sam was tense, and although Morgan had not even blinked when she had called him darling, she was worrying over what attitude he'd assume when meeting Mary and Deb. She glanced at him quickly. He looked healthy and full of vitality and altogether too handsome in a tan suit with a white and brown striped silk shirt, the white contrasting sharply with the dark brown of his face and throat. *The wretched man hasn't even the grace to look tired,* she thought peevishly, and felt her cheeks grow warm remembering the night before. Catching her look, Morgan arched a brow and grinned wickedly at her as if he'd read her thoughts.

Her tension mounting, Sam gave a sigh of relief, wanting to have it over with, when the big car turned into the drive and slowed to a stop in front of the big house.

"Very elegant," Morgan said softly, stepping out of the car and turning to help Sam before Dave had cut the engine.

As Sam stepped from the car, the front door opened and

105

a small, dark-haired figure ran lightly down the steps and in a soft, lilting voice cried, "Sam," as she hurtled herself into Sam's arms.

Sam hugged her half sister, then held her away from her, laughing softly. "Poppet, you're looking positively radiant."

"Oh, Sam, I've missed you so much. It's seemed like ages," Deb said softly and Sam felt the breath catch in her throat, for Deb had tears in her eyes. Then Deb turned, an unsure look on her face, and tilted her head way back to look at Morgan, who had stood quietly watching. She put her hand out slowly. "Morgan?"

Morgan took her hand into his, and Sam was astonished at the look of tenderness on his face as he said gently, "I've never had a sister, Deb, but if I had, I'd want her to be just like you, small and dark and captivating." He paused, then added, "Will you be my sister, Deb?"

Sam watched, some of the tension inside her lessening, as the unsure look on Deb's face changed to one of enchantment. "I'd love to be your sister, Morgan," Deb answered, a radiant smile curving her lips.

Stepping forward, Morgan let go of Deb's hand to scoop her off her feet and into his arms, kissing her soundly on the mouth.

"Don't enjoy that too much, Deb." The pleasant warning came from Bryan as he came slowly down the steps.

Morgan sat a laughing Deb back on her feet and she turned to Bryan, who came to a stop next to her. "Darling, this is Morgan and as he is my new brother, you must be nice to him."

"As long as he doesn't make a habit of kissing you," he answered dryly, looking up at Morgan, who stood a good four inches taller than he did. The two men eyed each other silently a few seconds, each taking the other's measure, then seemed to reach a decision simultaniously as both grinned and put forth a hand.

"Bryan."

"Morgan."

Bryan turned to Sam and Morgan saw the same warm look in his eyes that he'd seen in Dave's as he murmured almost the exact same words. "Welcome home, Sam."

"Hello, Pet." Smiling, Sam walked into his outstretched arms.

Morgan's voice was as dry as Bryan's had been a few moments ago. "As long as you don't make a habit of that, Bryan."

Laughing easily together, the four mounted the steps and entered the house. The feeling of ease left Sam abruptly when, once inside the large hall, Deb said, "Mother's waiting in the small sitting room, Sam." Arm in arm, she and Bryan walked in the direction of that room.

Sam's steps faltered and without saying anything or even looking at her, Morgan took her hand, entwined his fingers in hers and drew her along behind the other couple.

"Settle down, Red," he drawled softly. "I promise I won't let you down. Be a good girl and your family will be as ignorant of our deception when we leave as they are right now."

Sam shot a startled, uneasy glance at him, but they were at the sitting room doorway before she could form a reply.

As they entered the room, Mary stood, hands outstretched, saying in her sweet, cultured voice, "Samantha, darling, I can't tell you how good it is to see you and have you home again."

Morgan loosened his hold. Steps hurrying now, Sam went to Mary, put her hands in hers and, bending, kissed her soft cheek. "And it's wonderful to be here with you, Mother." Then, turning, "Here's Morgan."

Her stepmother was delicate and sometimes seemed a trifle vague, but everyone in the house knew that very little escaped her attention. So Sam held her breath as Morgan, bending over the petite woman, enclosed her tiny hand in his large one. "I'm happy to meet you, finally, Mrs. Denning. May I call you Mary?" On her nod, he continued. "Though I could hardly believe her, you are every bit as lovely as Sam said you were."

Mary's cheeks pinked becomingly. "How charming you are." Her eyes dancing, she added, "And I'm afraid a bit of a rogue."

Morgan grinned, his black eyes laughing. "You won't tell anyone, will you?"

Mary's soft, sweet laughter floated through the air. "I hardly think that will be necessary, my dear. Now, I'm sure you both want to freshen up. Samantha, dear, you're in your own room, of course. Take Morgan up and join us for lunch whenever you're ready."

Sam closed the door gently behind her, watching Morgan as he sauntered into her room, his eyes missing nothing. "Thank you," she whispered.

He turned slowly, his eyes pinning her to the door. "What for?"

"For being so nice to them. They're very important to me."

His voice was very low. "I know that. It was easy to be nice to them, they're very nice people." His voice took on an edge. "For God's sake, Sam, what did you expect me to do?"

She shrugged helplessly, despite his words earlier, she had been worried. "I don't know, but, I was afraid." Her breath caught; she could say no more.

His eyes mocked her, his voice was impatient. "I know

108

that too. Five months and you don't know me at all, do you, Redhead?"

She straightened, moving away from the door. She was home, in her own room and she was determined, no matter how much she loved him, he would not intimidate her here. "I know you as well as I care to," she said coolly, walking to the bathroom. Her hand on the doorknob, his laughing voice stopped her.

"It won't work, Samantha."

Sam felt a small shiver trickle down her stiff spine. Forcing her voice to remain cool, she snapped. "I don't know what you mean."

His laughter deepened, as did his voice. "No? I think you do. Planning to put me in my place while we're here, aren't you? You won't, but have fun trying, Redhead, because I'm going to enjoy watching you."

She spun around, her eyes blazing and without taking time to think, bit out, "You really are an arrogant bastard, aren't you?" She stopped, appalled at herself.

He was across the room in a few strides, gripping her shoulders painfully, his eyes and voice hard with anger.

"Is that how you think of me?"

"Morgan, I'm sorry."

"Don't ever be sorry for saying what you think to me. I'm your husband and regardless of what you think of me, we have a bargain and you'll stick to it." The anger seemed to drain out of him and dropping his hands to his sides he said calmly, "We don't want to keep your family waiting too long for their lunch." Pulling the bathroom door open for her he added, "Don't be too long—darling."

Sam's hands shook as she washed her face and applied fresh makeup lightly. She was more frightened of him when he was cool and calm than when he was angry.

Sam's nerves grew taut over the next few days. She felt like she was living with two different people. When they were alone in the bedroom, Morgan was reserved, withdrawn. He barely spoke to her and for the first time since he'd carried her to his bed and made her his, he didn't touch her at night. When they were with other people he was charming and attentive, the endearments coming smoothly and easily from his mouth.

Mary and Deb had told no one they were coming, wanting to have Sam to themselves for the few days before the party. Sam and Morgan spent those days horseback riding with Deb and Bryan or lazing by the pool, for all the world like a happy family group.

By Friday morning Sam felt slightly sick with apprehension. Morgan would be meeting her friends for the first time at the party and she wondered nervously what they would think of him and, more importantly, what he would think of them.

Sam found herself alone soon after breakfast, Mary and Deb having gone shopping for some last-minute items for the party. Morgan was gone when she woke and hadn't returned for breakfast. Restlessly she paced her room, then, grabbing up her purse, she left the room and ran down the steps. She'd go for a drive. Always before, whenever she was upset, she drove alone, and it had always soothed her, calmed her down. She hadn't driven her car since coming home, hadn't even looked at it, and now as she left the house by a side door and hurried along the graveled walk to the row of garages in back, she was eager to get behind the wheel again. Although she knew that Dave would have kept her car in perfect running condition, it would probably do it good if she gave it a good run.

Hurrying along, head bent, Sam was deep in thought, remembering the last time she'd had to let off tension by driving alone. She'd quarreled bitterly with her father. Over what? She couldn't remember, but she remembered leaving the house in anger and driving, much too fast, for over an hour. When she'd returned, the anger was gone and she'd calmly gone to her father and smoothed over their argument. Two weeks later he was dead and she was thankful now that she'd—

"Going somewhere, Redhead?" Morgan's voice cut across her thoughts, and she stopped, startled, looking up quickly. He stood leaning against the Cadillac parked in front of the garage.

"I didn't hear the car," Sam said in confusion. He'd been riding and Sam's eyes ran the length of him. He wore flat-heeled boots and his long legs and slim hips were encased in tight black jeans. A white shirt open at the throat, sleeves rolled to the elbow, was an assault on the eyes in the bright morning sunlight. Within seconds every detail about him registered in her mind. The gold watch gleaming against the dark skin on his wrist, the narrow platinum band on his finger, the crisp black hair, the ends given a silvery look by the sunlight. His eyes were hidden from her by large wire-framed sunglasses, and his mouth, sensuous, the lips perfectly outlined, which could become suddenly straight and hard, now curved in mild amusement.

Sam took him all in and was shattered emotionally. As she moved, began walking toward him, she admitted to herself that the only thing on this earth she wanted was to walk up to him, slide her arms around that slim waist, fasten her mouth to his and feel the long, lean hardness of his body against hers. Her thoughts brought her up short, and she eyed him in resentment. Why, why, of all the men she'd met, did it have to be this one? This cowboy who looked at her in contemptuous amusement.

"I've been here awhile." His voice was pure silk. "And I asked you a question."

Anger burned through her. Who the hell did he think he was? Her voice frosty, she said, "I'm going for a drive."

"Dave driving?"

"Of course not! I'm taking my car." Sam ground her teeth as she watched one black brow arch above the rim of his sunglasses.

"I'll go with you," he said softly.

"No," she almost shouted the word at him.

The tone lowered, became a soft purr. "I said I'll go with you."

Sam glared at him, then stormed into the garage, slid behind the wheel and backed the red Stingray out of its stall.

Now both brows peeked over the glass rims and as Morgan folded himself into the seat next to her, he murmured, "Nice little toy you have here."

She smiled sweetly at him. "I hope you're comfortable —darling."

Morgan grinned at her and in fury she tore along the drive and onto the road and for the next thirty minutes drove like the demons of hell were tailgating her. He sat silent until she had ripped back up the driveway and into the stall, stopping the car a bare half inch from the back wall. Watching her, his attitude one of complete boredom, he removed his sunglasses, held them by one earpiece between thumb and forefinger and gently swung them back and forth. "Feel better now, Redhead?" he drawled. Bending and leaning to her, he kissed her lightly on the lips.

His utter indifference exploded the already seething anger inside her. Sam didn't think, she reacted. Her hand flew up and across his face, then back to her mouth. In horror at what she'd done, she watched his eyes and face go hard. The red mark of her fingers growing on his cheek, he said coldly, "You're behaving like a very spoiled little girl, Samantha, and I'm getting a little sick of it. Be very careful you don't twist the tiger's tail too hard, or you're liable to find you've started something you can't finish."

Sam sat rigid as, without looking at her again, Morgan slid his body up the back of the seat to an almost standing position and stepped over and out of the car.

Although she felt rather sick, with nerves fluttering in her stomach, Sam managed a small salad at lunch, but begged off dinner, claiming a headache, promising Mary she'd have a nap before the party. In fact she did fall asleep after swallowing two aspirin and stretching out across the bed. She woke to find Morgan already showered and getting dressed. Without a word she entered the bathroom, taking an extra long time over her bath and applying her makeup until, relief washing over her, she heard the bedroom door close behind him.

She entered the now empty bedroom, stepped into lacy white briefs and gold evening sandals. She brushed her hair into deliberately wild and disordered curls around her face. She sprayed herself lavishly with a light, spicy perfume and, with more than a little trepidation, she went to her closet and removed her new gown, putting it on quickly before she could change her mind. Why had she bought it? she wondered, as she studied her reflection in the long mirror. It was not her usual style at all.

Of white lace, it contrasted perfectly with the beautiful golden glow her skin had acquired over the summer. But, she reflected, it revealed much too much skin. There was very little to the top of the dress, nothing at all to the back, being cut out like a large U from one shoulder to the other. The front had little more material as it plunged in a V

113

from her shoulders almost to her waist. The ends of her shoulders, about an inch, and her arms were covered, the sleeves of the dress being long and full. The cut of the gown gave her waist an even smaller look, and from the waist the material fit perfectly over her hips and fell straight to the floor, giving her a long, leggy look.

Sam shook her head slowly at her reflection. No, Morgan was definitely not going to approve. Glancing at the clock, she realized she was already late, so with a small shrug of her shoulders, she straightened her back, lifted her chin, and left the room.

Morgan was the first person Sam saw as she came slowly down the broad, curving staircase. He stood talking to Mary and some of Sam's friends, and as if he sensed her there on the stairs, he looked up, then went completely still. She saw a flicker of surprise go across his face and his eyes widen for an instant before narrowing. His reaction had lasted only seconds, but Sam knew he was angry, very angry. She continued to move down the stairs, her breath catching in her throat, as she watched Morgan murmur a few words to Mary and start toward her. He had taken a few strides, then stopped short, his face going hard, as a deep, caressing voice was raised above the normal tones of the other guests. "Sam, my love, if you intended to make an entrance, you've certainly succeeded. You look positively ravishing."

Sam saw Morgan turn sharply and walk away before she turned, at the bottom of the stairs now, and smilingly placed her hands into the outstretched ones of the owner of that deep voice.

Jeffrey Hampton was as handsome as ever. Tall and fair, his light hair gleaming in the brightly lit hall, he stood smiling at her, his eyes bright with admiration. Leaning to her, he kissed her gently on the mouth and said softly,

"It's great to see you again, angel, it's been a very dull summer with you not here."

Sam laughed up at him, but said in a stern voice, "Jeffrey Hampton, that's an awful thing for you to say, in view of the fact that you became engaged this summer."

"Oh, that," he shrugged lightly. "What has that to do with the fact that I still love you madly and missed you?"

Sam frowned. "Jeff, behave yourself." But she had to smile again at the quick impish grin he gave her. She had turned down his proposal of marriage twice, but even so had continued to go around with him. He was a charming, delightful companion and they had fun together.

Now she couldn't help comparing him with the man she'd married. As always, he was elegantly dressed, tonight in midnight-blue evening clothes, with a pale-blue shirt with ruffles at the front and wrists. As Jeff cupped her elbow with his hand and led her into the large room off the hall cleared of all furniture and full of laughing, talking people, she realized she hadn't even noticed what Morgan was wearing.

She glanced around quickly and saw him across the room standing in front of the fireplace, looking completely relaxed, with one arm resting against the mantelpiece, drink in hand, looking down at the young woman speaking to him. Sam's eyes went over him and, as before, the look of him did strange things to her legs and made her breath catch in her throat. His black evening clothes were perfectly cut to his long, lithe frame and along with his dark skin and black brows and hair, gave him a slightly satanic look. His white shirt and flashing white teeth, as he suddenly smiled, looked startling against all that darkness. Her eyes shifted to the woman he'd smiled at—Jeff's newly acquired fiancée, Carolyn Henkes.

Sam had never liked Carolyn overmuch and now, as she

watched her flutter long, pale-gold lashes up at Morgan, she decided she liked her even less. That Carolyn was a beauty, Sam would not deny. With long white-gold hair that framed a beautiful pink and white heartshaped face, out of which gazed large cornflower-blue eyes, she was as lovely as an exquisite china doll and, Sam knew, just as brittle. She could be delightful and sweet, but equally biting and vicious if she thought her interests were threatened. Morgan, Sam noted with dismay, seemed captivated by her.

She heard Jeff chuckle close to her ear and knew his eyes had followed hers as he whispered, "It would seem my intended is quite taken with your somewhat overpowering husband."

A few minutes later, as the music started, Sam felt Morgan's arm slide around her waist, heard him drawl softly, "I think we're to have the first dance—darling." He led her to the cleared area at the end of the long room. His appearance was that of the happy, devoted bridegroom as he drew her into his arms and bent his smiling face to her. But Sam felt cold apprehension go through her, for every muscle in his body was tense with anger and his voice, in her ear, whispered harshly, "What the hell are you trying to prove with that dress?"

CHAPTER 7

Some six hours later Sam entered her room and stood rigid, fists at her sides, her back to the door. She knew there was an angry argument about to follow her and, sighing deeply, she moved into the room, kicking her sandals off as she went. The white shag rug felt good to her tired feet and she stood still, in the center of the room, curling her toes against the soft fibers. She felt tired and slightly lightheaded. She had eaten very little all day and had had far too much champagne, as she had seemed to acquire an almost unquenchable thirst after that first dance.

The party had been torment for her. Morgan had barely talked to her after that first dance and yet he had managed to give the impression of their being the happy newlyweds as he moved about the room meeting her friends. He had danced with all the women and stood and talked with all the men, occasionally giving her one of his devastating white smiles. But his eyes did not smile and Sam could see the fury glittering in them across the width of the room. She had not been the one at his side, making the introductions. Carolyn, smiling up at him and hanging onto his arm like a growth, had performed that duty for her, occasionally casting Sam a smug, malicious glance.

Jeff had been her shadow all evening. As she had moved

about, forcing herself to talk and laugh with her friends, he had become increasingly more familar, dropping his arm first about her shoulders, then around her waist. Each time he danced with her his hand grew more bold, caressing her exposed back. Sam had told him warningly to stop when he had slid his fingers under the material and along her side. She had given her warning softly, not wanting to draw attention to herself. Jeff had laughed at her and, taking her hand, had drawn her through the french windows into the garden. The garden had been transformed into a make-believe place of moving lights and shadows by the strings of patio lights draped from tree to tree for the party. There were couples dancing on the grass just outside the doors and Jeff kept moving deeper into the garden along the hedge-lined path away from the glow of the lights. He had stopped suddenly and, without a word, pulled her into his arms and kissed her.

Sam stood passive a few moments. Jeff's kiss, as always before, was pleasant, but it struck no response from her. When she didn't respond, Jeff's lips became more demanding and Sam pulled herself free and walked away from him, deeper into the shadows. She had walked a short distance when she stopped, then, turning quickly, hurried back to Jeff, and in a voice barely controlling her anger, told him she wanted a drink. He didn't argue, thinking her anger directed at him, but followed her quietly into the house.

Sam brought the wineglass to her lips, amazed at the intensity of her feelings. Her hands were shaking and she drained the glass quickly and put it down before anyone noticed. Pain tore through her as a picture of what she had seen flashed across her mind. Carolyn, smiling face upturned, one arm stretched out, fingers touching his cheek. Morgan, white teeth flashing in his dark face as he bent over her, his big hands closing on her shoulders. It had taken every ounce of will power Sam possessed to turn away and walk back to the house. She had wanted to scream and fly at Carolyn's face with her nails. Somehow she managed to get through what was left of the evening without giving herself away. Now, as she stood absolutely still in the middle of her room, her nails dug into her palms and she felt her back stiffen. She had been sure he saw other women when away, but to actually see him, here!

Sam froze as the door opened, then closed quietly. The long silent moment drew her nerves taut and she spun angrily at his softly grated, "Get that goddamned rag off before I do it for you."

Her mouth open to argue, the words died in Sam's throat when she looked at him. The look of him frightened her. He leaned lazily against the door, and she thought wildly that he looked like some huge cat ready to pounce on her. She had never seen him this angry and, although his voice had been soft, she could see he was fighting to control himself. His face seemed carved in stone and his eyes, which could look hard and cold as black ice, now blazed at her in fury.

Sam found her voice and even managed to keep it cool. "You have no right to speak to me like that."

His purred answer drew fingers of ice down her spine. "You have thirty seconds."

Sam stared at him. This didn't make sense. All this fury over a gown? She lifted her head even higher, cool green eyes matched her tone, giving away nothing of the unease she felt. "Morgan, I don't think I understand what this is all about."

"No?" Eyes narrowing, he moved toward her. Her pose of cool indifference seemed to unleash the heat inside him. The purr took on a very rough edge. "Then I'll tell you what it's all about. That dress is an open invitation to all comers." As she opened her mouth to protest, he snarled harshly, "Don't interrupt. You're my wife, Samantha, my woman, you use my name. And what wears my brand is mine. I don't share my wealth."

All composure gone, voice rising, Sam cried, "Wears your brand? Morgan, I'm a person, not part of your stock."

"I never said you were, but that ring you wear is my brand and as long as you wear it, you're mine." Voice low, menacing he added, "And if your pretty boyfriend ever puts his hands on you again I'll drop him. Now get that damn dress off."

Sam winced as if the words he rapped out at her actually struck her. Turning her back, she put trembling fingers to the small zipper at the back of her waist and tugged. She drew the sleeves from her arms and the dress slid from her to the floor, forming a circle around her feet. In defiance, she stepped outside that circle and kicked the garment across the room. Standing straight and stiff, the lacy panties her only covering, she heard a low humorless chuckle behind her and, eyes wide, watched his jacket, shirt and tie arch through the air and land on top of her gown.

"No," Sam whispered, her shaking hand reaching for the nightgown lying across the foot of the bed next to which she stood.

Morgan's hand closed around her wrist; his voice was a harsh whisper in her ear. "Did you enjoy the feel of pretty boy's hands and lips, Samantha?"

His words hurt. A picture of him bending over Carolyn flashed through her mind, and that hurt even more. She wanted to hurt back, and giving no thought to her nudity, she wrenched her arm from his hand and turned on him hotly. "You bloody beast. How dare you? Jeff's an old friend and he loves me. He's gentle and considerate and I should have married him when he asked me." She was lashing out blindly, not pausing to think, trying to inflict on him a small measure of the pain she had felt tear through her in the garden. "I'll see him whenever I wish and if I want to go to bed with him, I shall. He at least doesn't want my money." Pulling his rings from her finger, she threw them at his face. "And you can take your brand and you can—"

The words died on her lips for, after throwing the rings, she had tossed back her head and seen his face. Real fear crawled through her stomach as his hands gripped her shoulders painfully. "You redheaded witch," he gritted between clenched teeth. "You try and put horns on me with Hampton and I'll take him apart—slowly. Do you understand that?"

Sam nodded dumbly, unable to take her eyes from his savage face, fighting the panic growing inside. Releasing her shoulders he stepped back. "Pick your rings up and put them on. Now."

It was a command, and without question she hurried to obey. But a spark of defiance made her say as she straightened, sliding the rings into place, "May I please go to bed now?"

The grin he gave her was wicked as, cupping her chin in his hand, he bent his head to hers and said mockingly, "I thought you'd never ask."

Sam jerked her head away as his mouth touched hers. "No, Morgan, it's late and I'm very tired, I want—"

"Too bad." His words cut across hers like a steel blade. "I warned you to be careful not to twist the tiger's tail too hard. You had to see just how far you could go, didn't you, Red?" He pulled her against him, his mouth hard, demanding, hurting hers.

121

The sound of his voice, his unbridled rage, frightened Sam and she fought him. She kicked him, hit out with her hands balled into fists and she tore at his hair.

His face grim, set, he picked her up and dumped her onto the bed. She lay sprawled, gasping for breath, her eyes wide with shock, watching him as he stripped off the rest of his clothes. Rolling over she tried to jump from the other side of the bed, but Morgan dropped down beside her, and his arm shot out and around her waist, dragging her back against him. She fought like a wild thing, twisting and arching her body away from him, hitting, kicking. She cursed him in a raw, breathless hiss and he laughed at her. Twice she was rewarded for her efforts when she heard him grunt in pain, deep in his throat. Once when her nails raked across his cheek, again when her teeth drew blood from his shoulder. She couldn't win and she knew it, but she also knew she'd put up a good fight, for his dark skin glistened as wetly as hers and the hair around his face was as damp as her own. She lay quiet, finally, drawing great gulps of air into her lungs, her eyes still rebellious and stormy on his.

"You're really beautiful, Redhead," he whispered as he lowered his face to hers. Then, his lips brushing hers, "And a magnificent adversary, but you lose." His mouth took hers in a kiss that robbed her of all breath and all reason. It was full daylight before he moved away from her to lay on his back breathing deeply, his eyes closed.

Sam lay beside him, the back of her hand pressed against her mouth, fighting, in vain, against the tears that rolled down her temple and into her hair. She was filled with shame and disgust, but with herself, not him. That she loved him she'd faced months ago, but how deep, how intense within her that love went was borne upon her now.

His lovemaking had been almost savage, and she'd been

122

lost from that first kiss. She'd matched his savagery with her own, obeying his commands willingly, eagerly. There was not a spot on her body that his hands and mouth did not now know, and she'd trembled in delight at their knowing. He'd bid her own to explore him, and she'd gloried in their knowledge. Yet he'd as much as told her she was a possession, part of his property, to be used when he needed, like his house, or his plane, or his horse. She felt wounded and lacerated almost beyond endurance.

He turned his head and looked at her, then sighing deeply, in what she was sure was disgust, he left the bed and went into the bathroom. She heard the water running in the shower just before she fell asleep.

When she woke it was mid-afternoon and she was alone. She lay for some time reliving the night before, then, with a deep sigh, she got up. She wanted nothing as much as she wanted to pull the sheet over her head and never leave her bed again.

Before showering she stood and studied her nude form carefully in the mirror. Again she sighed. She was beginning to have an angular look. She had always been slim, but now, with the weight she'd lost, she looked almost skinny. But this fact she barely noticed, for all she saw were the bruises Morgan had left on her. It had been a fierce battle. Morgan had not been playing with her. Even her legs had not escaped the marks from his hands. At the thought of those hands she twisted around and went into the bathroom.

Sam had dressed in slacks and longsleeved shirt and was sitting at her dresser brushing her hair when Morgan came into the room carrying a tray. Her eyes, guarded, wary, met his in the mirror. Lifting the tray in a wry salute, he arched a brow, murmured sardonically, "From Beth, with orders to eat all of it." He walked across the room and set the tray on the table by the windows, then stretched out in the chair next to it.

"I'm really not hungry." Sam went back to her brushing.

"It's two o'clock, you've eaten practically nothing for over twenty-four hours, Samantha. Come over here and eat something." His voice held a lazy drawl. It also held an order.

Flinging the brush down, she spun around, eyes blazing, ready to argue. The sight of his face stopped the words in her throat. He lay back in the chair, eyes closed, looking incredibly tired. He had a pinched, drawn look, the welts her fingernails had made red and angry looking across his cheek.

She had seen him after weeks of working fourteen- and sixteen-hour days, and he had never looked like this. *What are we doing to each other?* she thought tiredly. All fight and anger drained out of her. She walked to the table and sat in the chair across from him. The tray held a pot of coffee, two fat mugs and a covered plate, which held bacon, eggs, and two toasted English muffins dripping with butter.

Sam filled both mugs with coffee and sat watching Morgan, gnawing on her lip. He had obviously been riding, as he wore boots, jeans, and a blue cotton shirt, the sleeves rolled up to his elbows. "Your coffee's getting cold." She said the words softly, not sure if he'd fallen asleep. At the sound of her voice he slid his body up in the chair and opened his eyes, one brow going up in question at the look on her face. She lowered her eyes, stammered "I—I'm sorry about your face."

The soft laugh had the sound of bitterness, not humor. "You're some tigress, Redhead." He nodded at the tray. "Eat something, Samantha, then I want to talk to you."

124

Reaching a hand to the tray, he murmured, "May I?" He picked up a piece of the muffin at her nod.

He sat munching the muffin, watching her as she forced down a piece of bacon and some of the eggs. When she sat back in her chair, her mug cradled in her hands, he said, "Finished?" Sam nodded, watched his fingers smooth over the welts on his cheek. "I told Mary I rode too close to a tree branch. So if anyone asks, you know what to say. Unless, of course, there's someone you'd like to tell the truth to."

"Morgan, please."

He smiled slightly at the note of reproach in her voice and went on. "Well, then, Mary tells me we've received quite a few invitations, beginning with a dinner dance at the club tonight and varied other things right through the weekend. You had remembered that this is the Labor Day weekend?" At her brief nod he continued. "I told her, for my part, she should accept any of these invitations she wished, but I'd send you to confer with her on the matter. Okay?"

"Yes, of course."

He drank his coffee, held the mug out for her to refill it, before going on. "Now the important part. I like your family very much, Samantha, and I see no reason why we should worry them with our marital difficulties. So I suggest we call a truce. At least for the remainder of our visit."

"You mean to take me with you then, when you go home?" Her voice was low, but she had managed to keep it steady.

Morgan had bent his head to his mug, but at her words his head jerked up, his eyes going hard and cold. "Are you trying to tell me you're not going with me?" Before she could answer, he added, his voice very soft, "Maybe you're thinking of ending this marriage."

The last thing in the world I want is to end our marriage, her mind cried. Aloud she replied carefully, "I thought, perhaps, you were thinking along those lines."

He looked at her a long time through narrowed lids before answering shortly, "You know that's impossible under the circumstances, don't you?"

"Yes," she whispered.

He gave her a strange look, then rapped, "All right then, do you agree to a truce?" When she again whispered, "Yes," he stood and completely surprised her by bending over her and brushing his lips across hers. Straightening, he began to unbutton his shirt. "Do you have any plans for what's left of the afternoon?"

"Yes. I have a friend who runs a boutique not far from here and I thought I'd run over and do some shopping. Why? Did you have something you wanted to do?"

He threw her a wicked grin. "Yes, I'm going to take a shower and have a nap until it's time to dress for dinner. Too bad you can't join me."

"In which?" Sam retorted.

His grin widened. "In both. Are you going to be shopping for something to wear tonight?"

"Yes, why?" She eyed him warily, thinking their truce would be short-lived if he tried to tell her what to buy.

He was tugging his shirt from his jeans as he answered. "Get something in white. Although I didn't approve of your dress last night, I have to admit that with the tan you've acquired you look pretty terrific in white." Without waiting for her to comment, he turned, pulling his shirt off, toward the bathroom.

Sam's eyes widened when she saw his back, for, although they were longer, the red, angry-looking welts

126

crisscrossing his back exactly matched those on his face. How could she have done something like that? she thought as a small gasp escaped through the fingers that had flown to her mouth.

On hearing her gasp, Morgan turned quickly. "What is it?" Sam's eyes widened even more at the ugly mark her teeth left on his shoulder.

He frowned and his voice sounded concerned. "Sam, what is wrong?"

"Oh, Lord, Morgan, your back—your shoulder. Do you think you should have a tetanus shot?"

With that he laughed aloud in real amusement. "No, I don't, my redheaded tigress, I get T shots regularly and I doused myself with antiseptic this morning and I will again after I've showered, so stop looking so scared. Run along and enjoy your shopping." Still laughing softly he turned and strode into the bathroom.

Sam did enjoy her shopping. After a short consultation with Mary, during which she agreed to all plans for the weekend, she and a very willing Deb made the short run to the small shop. She and Jean, the woman who ran the shop, spent a few minutes catching up on news of each other, Jean exclaiming over Sam's ring, then the three women got down to the serious business of clothes for Sam's slimmer figure. She bought slacks and a few skirts, tops, and three long gowns, one in white, even though she'd told herself she wouldn't. Then telling Jean they'd see her at the club, they went back to the house and right to their rooms, as it was time to get ready for dinner.

Morgan was still sprawled out on the bed asleep when Sam got back and her eyes kept straying to his sleeping face as she moved around the room quietly, hanging her clothes away. Relaxed, his face had lost the tight, drawn look and in turn seemed less grim and hard.

She slid silently into the bathroom and was standing in brief panties and bra in front of the bathroom mirror, some fifteen minutes later, making her face up, when the door opened and he leaned against the frame watching her.

Raising the eye shadow applicator to her lid, she lifted her eyes, caught the look on his face reflected in the mirror, and repeated his words of that afternoon. "What is it?"

He stretched out an arm and his fingertips touched gently at the large, purpling bruise on her arm. Then his hand dropped to her hip where another bruise was partially covered by her panties. Giving a light tug at the elastic, he exposed it in all its colorful size. His eyes went over her slowly, noting all the marks on her. As his eyes came back to her face, he raised his finger to her cheek, gently caressing it. His voice deep and husky with emotion, he said, "And you were concerned about me!" His other hand lifted her arm and drew her toward him as he bent his head. Pressing his lips gently to the bruise on her arm he murmured, "I'm sorry, Sam, I had no right to do this to you. You have my word that it won't happen again."

Taken completely by surprise by this gentleness he'd never shown to her before, Sam's reply sounded cold and stiff. "All right, Morgan, now we'd really better get ready as it's getting late."

"Of course." His hands dropped and he stepped back abruptly.

She noticed, for the first time, that he was already partially dressed, lacking only shirt, tie and jacket. Scooping up her makeup she slipped by him. "I'll leave you to shave."

She had finished her makeup and was struggling with the long zipper at the back of her gown when he reentered

128

the room. Standing as if fascinated, he watched her a few seconds, until she snapped in agitation, "Don't just stand there for heaven's sake, help with this blasted thing." His lips twitching, he walked up behind her and with one tug closed the zipper. Stepping back he ordered, "Turn around."

She turned around slowly as he took in the white sheath. It was simply cut and fitted snugly, with long close-fitting sleeves and a low, square neckline, but not too low. The tight skirt was slit to the knees on both sides.

"Very nice. Now stand still," he murmured, going to the dresser and taking a case from the top drawer. As he walked back to her, he opened the case and removed a necklace from it, then, flipping the case onto the bed, he stood behind her and clasped the chain around her neck. Sam went to the mirror and stared at the large diamond-encircled emerald that hung at the end of the platinum chain.

"But why?"

"Call it a belated wedding gift." He shrugged, went to the closet, pulled out a white silk shirt, muttered brusquely, "Now say thank you and get the hell out of here, so I can get dressed." Hesitantly, she went to him, gave him a quick kiss, mumbled "thank you," and hurried from the room, not understanding him at all.

The evening passed pleasantly enough, the only sour note as far as Sam was concerned was Carolyn's obvious interest in Morgan, and the fact that Morgan seemed to return that interest. Even Deb, who had decided Morgan was just about perfect, looked from one to the other, then to Sam with raised eyebrows.

During the next few days Sam felt the admiration and respect she already had for Morgan growing steadily. She knew he worked very hard, giving little time to relaxation and games, and yet, in the company of wealthy young men who made games their vocation, he adjusted quite well. He joined Bryan and two others in a round of golf and finished with a score only slightly higher than Bryan's, who was considered by far the best golfer in the district. He played a hard, fast game of tennis, with a serve that shot across the net like a missile. Sam had once before witnessed his swimming ability, the powerful strokes propelling his body swiftly through the water. She now found he could surf well and sail a small boat expertly. But it was when he stepped into the saddle that he put them all in the shade. All of her large group of friends rode well, the women as well as the men, but with Morgan, it was a part of his life. He seemed to become one with any horse from the moment he mounted, and no matter how difficult the animal, left no doubt as to who was the master.

They went to casual luncheons and cookouts and a formal dinner party at the home of Jeff's parents. At a wild, late-night poolside party Morgan stunned Sam by cutting in on Jeff and executing perfectly some very intricate dance steps. As the days slid by, Sam found herself becoming more and more withdrawn and rigid, for every time she'd look around for Morgan, she saw Carolyn hanging on his arm, and the look of concern growing in Deb's eyes. Deb, Sam knew, might be crazy about her new brother-in-law, but she adored Sam and she was worried.

They were at the breakfast table the Thursday following Sam's birthday party when Morgan was called to the phone. He took the call in her father's study, which he had commandeered as his own, making long phone calls and doing an endless amount of paper work whenever he had a few free minutes and late into the night. As before he put in sixteen-hour days.

He was in the study about ten minutes when he came out, barked "Sam" and went up the stairs two at a time.

Sam finished her coffee, lifted her shoulders in an I-don't-know to the questions in Mary's and Deb's eyes, and followed him up the stairs. When she entered their room she stopped cold. Morgan had their cases open on the bed, and was packing his own.

"What—" she began, but he cut her off.

"Something's come up, Samantha, that needs my personal attention. We've got to leave. I've already phoned to have the plane ready. I'll take you home, grab a few things I need, and take off." He turned back to the open dresser drawer.

Sam didn't move. When he turned around, hands full of clothes, he raised his eyebrows at her.

"How long will you be gone?" she asked softly.

"A week, ten days maybe," he shrugged. "I'm not sure. Why?"

Making up her mind suddenly, she answered, "Couldn't I stay here?" Before he could protest she hurried on. "Deb's wedding isn't too many weeks off, you know, and we have gown fittings and shopping to do. Morgan, we don't even have a wedding gift for them yet. Couldn't you come back here when you've completed your business?"

He looked at her hard and long before answering. "All right, Samantha, but don't shop for a wedding gift till I get back, we'll do that together. And, Redhead, behave yourself while I'm away." He laughed at the startled look she gave him. "Now come help me pack so I can get moving." It seemed he was gone in no time, and Sam was left with a strange, empty feeling.

The following day Sam and Deb were having lunch at the club when Jeff dropped into the chair next to Sam and said in mock forlornness, "Would you ladies allow a deserted man to join you for lunch?"

"Of course," Sam smiled. "But why deserted?"

His eyes danced devilishly. "My beloved left yesterday afternoon to visit with an aunt in Maine and I'm on my own for a week or so. And, as I understand you're also on your own, I was thinking, perhaps, we could be on our own together."

Sam had not missed the sharp look Deb had turned on her when Jeff said Carolyn had left so soon after Morgan and she felt slightly sick, but she managed to keep her voice light. "Sorry, Jeff, but Deb and I were just now making plans. You see, we have hours of shopping and fittings for the wedding and it's going to be a rush to get finished before Morgan gets back."

His handsome face wore a look of disappointment. "Oh, well, some days you can't win any of them."

Somehow Sam got through lunch, even managing to laugh at Jeff's mild jokes, but she drove home in silence, refusing to acknowledge Deb's worried glances. At the house she went straight to her room to pace back and forth with one thought. Had Morgan taken Carolyn with him? It seemed too much a coincidence, their leaving within a few hours of each other.

With a soft knock Deb entered, said hesitatingly, "Sam, darling—" but she got no further as Sam whispered, "Don't ask, Deb, please."

Sam was miserable. Although she went shopping and had fittings and oohed and aahed over incoming wedding gifts, one thought tormented her. Is he with her? She alternated between anger with and love for him and felt disgust with herself for her own weakness. She ate less than usual and lost more weight. She felt numb inside while maintaining an outward composure. She heard nothing from him.

Two weeks after Morgan left, Deb told her quietly that Carolyn had returned. Two days later Morgan came home.

In Mary's sitting room in front of the others, he drew her into his arms and kissed her. But once alone in the bedroom, he looked her over critically. "What kind of hours have you been keeping, Redhead?" he growled. "You look like hell."

"Thanks a lot," Sam snapped. Put out because he was looking so well, she slammed out of the room. They had almost three tense weeks together before he was gone again, not to return until the week before Deb's wedding.

Sam hadn't been feeling well since the middle of September, and when she began being sick to her stomach in the morning, then missed her second period, she faced the fact that she was pregnant. She had mixed feelings about it. She wanted Morgan's baby very badly, but she was beginning to believe he wanted out of their marriage. By the time Deb's wedding was over, they were barely on speaking terms, though they put on a good front in public.

The day after the wedding Morgan told her to pack. "We're going home. I have to go to Spain tomorrow."

"How long will you be gone?" she asked as she had weeks before.

His eyes and voice cold, he answered, "Ten days, possibly two weeks. Why? Aren't you coming with me again?"

"No, I'm not." At the look of anger that came into his face she added quickly, "I'm going home, Morgan, but I want to drive."

"Are you crazy?" he snapped. "I've seen you drive, remember? You'll come with me."

Growing angry herself now, Sam took her stand. "I do

133

not, as a rule, drive like that and I think you know it. I want my car."

"For God's sake why?" he grated, his eyes furious. "You have the Jag and the wagon at the ranch."

She held firm and to keep herself from shouting at him, she said through gritted teeth, "Morgan, I want my own car and I'm driving it to Nevada."

His eyes held hers a long moment, then he turned away sharply. "Do as you wish, I couldn't care less." Without another word he packed and went, this time with no pretense of tender leavetaking. It seemed to Sam that all hope went with him. She had a horrible feeling of certainty that their strange relationship was over.

CHAPTER 8

That night Sam lay wide awake, her mind working furiously. Morgan had said he'd be gone about two weeks. It would take her, at most, a few days to drive to the ranch. If she waited until next week to leave, she'd be subjected to Deb's probing, concerned glances. Yet, if she left tomorrow or the following day, she'd have a week of Sara's sharp-eyed scrutiny. Neither prospect held much appeal.

Aunt Rachael! The name sprang into her mind out of the blue. Sam had received several letters from her favorite aunt, coaxing letters, asking her when she was coming to visit. On the spur of the moment Sam decided to fly to England and stay with her mother's sister for a week. And Morgan Wade could just go hang.

Arrangements were quickly made and two days later, much to the surprise of her family, Sam was on her way to England. On the plane the thought, belatedly, struck Sam that Morgan had never told her what the Messrs. Baker had wanted. With a shrug she dismissed it, too busy concentrating on not being airsick to worry about it now.

Rachael Crinshaw, tall, elegant, her auburn hair still glowingly beautiful, was waiting for Sam at the airport. After the general confusion of luggage collection and customs, they followed Rachael's chauffeur to her Mercedes.

When she was settled into the car, Sam let her head drop back wearily against the seat.

"Are you all right, Samantha?" Rachael asked in quick concern. "You are absolutely white and, to be perfectly honest, you look like a stick with material draped around it. I realize the fashions call for slimness, but don't you think you've carried it a bit far?"

"I'm fine, Aunt Rachael." Despite the tiredness dragging at her spirit, Sam smiled. "I haven't been dieting. The summer was so hot and humid I simply had no appetite. I'm sure I'll regain the weight now that summer is finally over." *In fact,* she thought wryly, *I'm positive of it.*

"Well, I should hope so," Rachael chided gently. "Really, dear, you look absolutely haggard. I fully intend supervising your meals while you're here. I can't imagine what that husband of yours is thinking of to allow you to reach this degree of—of gauntness."

"Oh, really, Aunt Rachael," Sam laughed a little unsurely. "Morgan has no control over what I eat. You, of all people, should know how I'd react if a man tried directing my life down to the food I put into my mouth."

At least the Samantha her aunt had known would never have allowed a man to direct her life, Sam thought ruefully, memories of the number of times Morgan had done just that making her squirm with discomfort.

Sam greeted the sight of her aunt's tall, imposing house with a sigh of relief. She was so tired her eyelids felt weighted with lead. Why was she always sleepy lately?

"If you don't mind, Aunt Rachael," Sam said, the minute they stepped into the large, formal hall. "I think I'd like to go right to my room and have a nap before dinner."

"Good idea." Rachael eyed her sharply. "I want to see some color back in your cheeks, my girl. Now, go along

136

with Claude and have a good rest. Dinner at seven, as usual."

With a wan smile Sam followed her aunt's very correct butler up the stairs. When she came down again three hours later, Rachael ran a critical eye over her, before declaring, "Much, much better. You are still pale, but the tight, pinched look is gone. Really, my dear, I had no idea they led such a wild existence in Long Island. Indeed, I understood your stepmother, Mary, was a shy, timid woman."

"Oh, Aunt Rachael!" Sam laughed. "Mary is a shy, timid woman and I love her dearly." Sam went on to briefly outline the activities that had been planned for her and Morgan. "Quite a few were held outdoors and, as I mentioned earlier, the heat really bothers me. I assure you I am fine."

Finally convinced, Rachael smiled warmly. "Good. I've been very busy since you called, Samantha. As I know how flying makes you sleepy, I planned a quiet dinner tonight, but I've invited quite a few of your friends for dinner tomorrow night."

"Oh, but Aunt Rachael—" Sam began, the idea of not only having to act well when she felt so washed out, but also appear as the happy bride, daunting.

Her aunt didn't let her finish her protest. "You haven't been over here in ages, darling, and all your friends want to see you. Several in particular." Her brows arched expressively. "I reminded them that you are now a married woman."

The dinner party turned out to be much more of an ordeal than she could have anticipated, even though it started out well. On awakening that morning she had been pleasantly surprised to find no sign of the gripping nausea or wracking sickness that had dogged her mornings for the past few weeks.

She and Rachael spent a leisurely, relaxing day, Sam wondering at times about the almost smugly self-satisfied expression that periodically played across her aunt's face. As Rachael was not forthcoming about the reason for her inner pleasure, Sam went to her room to dress for dinner in a bemused, questioning frame of mind.

Her question was answered the minute she stepped into her aunt's large drawing room, for one figure seemed to stand out from the several guests already gathered there.

"Duds!"

Sam's cry of delighted surprise brought all heads around to see her run across the room and into the outstretched arms of a tall, husky, sandy-haired man.

"Duds! How in the world did you get here? You look marvelous. I thought you were in Australia?"

The man's arms, tightening in a bear hug, cut off the overlapping string of Sam's words.

"Slow up a bit, darling." Clear blue eyes, bright with laughter, gazed into green. "One question at a time, please. But first"—his strong face split into a grin—"let me return the compliment twice over. You look delicious. Let's have a kiss."

Sam's mouth was caught in a deep, warm kiss which she returned unhesitatingly, without restraint. Dudley Haverstone, or Duds as Sam had christened him, was the only young man she had ever been able to truly relax with. From her fifth year, when her mother had married Dudley's father, Duds had been her older brother, her teacher, and her tormenter.

"Hmm, you taste delicious too," Duds murmured when he'd released her lips. Although his tone was serious, his

138

eyes teased her as they'd always done. "And you had to go and get yourself tied to the formidable Morgan."

"You know Morgan?" Sam gasped, eyes widening.

"Doesn't everyone?" Duds drawled before adding, "well, perhaps there are a few who don't."

"But, Duds, how do—"

"Enough about the cowboy," Duds cut her off. "I want to hear about you." Taking her arm, he drew her toward the far end of the room, calling over his shoulder, "If you'll excuse us, Aunt Rachael? Sam and I will rejoin the party in a few minutes."

With an indulgent smile Rachael waved them away before turning back to her guests.

"I missed you, Sam." They were sitting close together on an elegantly covered love seat, hands clasped. All traces of his former teasing tone were gone from Duds's voice. His eyes studied Sam's face minutely. "Little sister, why are you so thin?" Real concern tinged his tone, and the beginning of anger. "Is he giving you a hard time? Or have you heard the rumors already?"

"Rumors?" Sam's throat closed with alarm, a stab of fear jabbed at her stomach. "What rumors?"

"Oh, bloody hell," Duds groaned softly. His hands tightened almost painfully on hers. "Forget I said that, love."

"What rumors, Duds?" Sam's voice had steadied, gone cold.

"Sam, don't," Duds pleaded. "It's only rumors, after all. I'm sorry. I—"

"Duds, please, tell me." Neither Sam's face, nor her tone revealed the anxiety she was feeling. "I'd rather hear it from you. I haven't talked to anyone but Aunt Rachael since I arrived yesterday and even if Aunt Rachael had heard something, she wouldn't tell me. You know all the people who are going to be here tonight. You also know there will be more than one willing to enlighten me."

Duds grimaced, but before he could say anything Sam hurried on. "Duds, help me. If I know what to expect, I can handle it."

"You're right, of course," Duds sighed, then his voice went hard, frustrated. "He has been seen, several times the last week or so, with the same woman. A few times in Italy and, a couple of nights ago, here."

"Here!" Sam couldn't hide her astonishment. "Morgan is in London?"

"You didn't know?" Duds eyes sharpened on her face. "You didn't come over to join him?"

Sam's head was shaking before he'd stopped speaking. "No," she whispered, "I thought he was in Spain."

"Spain? Then what was he doing in Italy?"

"I don't know," Sam laughed shakily. "I know very little of Morgan's business, Duds." She paused, telling herself to leave it at that, but she had to ask. "Do you know who the woman is?"

"No, love," Duds answered softly. "And neither did my informant. Sam, I think I'd better also tell you that the woman seemed very sure of herself and that he was being very attentive. At least that's the story I got."

A change in the buzz of conversation at the other end of the room caught Sam's attention and, glancing up, she felt her breath catch painfully at her throat. As if their speaking about him had conjured him up, Morgan stood in the wide doorway, looking cool and relaxed and shatter-ingly handsome in a silver-gray hand-tailored suit that, if possible, made his hair and eyes look even blacker.

With deadly accuracy those eyes honed in on Sam, paused a moment on her hands tightly clasped in Duds's before lifting to pierce hers, black fury raging in their depths.

"Morgan, darling, you're late."

Her aunt's melodious voice reached Sam's disbelieving ears and, shock waves rippling through her, she watched in astonishment as Rachael hurried across the room to him, lifted her cheek for his kiss. Did Rachael know him too then? Apparently, for Morgan murmured something that made her laugh, brushed a becoming tinge of pink across her cheeks.

Somehow Sam managed to conceal the tension mounting wildly inside. Looking cool, almost remote, she fought down the urge to run as Morgan nodded an encompassing greeting to the others before sauntering across the long room to where she sat with Duds.

Duds was on his feet before Morgan was halfway to them, right hand extended, left hand still clasping Sam's.

"Hello, Morgan, it's been a long time." Duds's voice, though friendly, held a note of wariness. "I'd heard you were in town."

"Dudley." Morgan's hand gripped Duds briefly. "When did you escape from the bush?"

"A week ago," Duds smiled fleetingly. "Although I only actually arrived in London two days ago."

"I see. The day before Samantha did." His voice was smooth, his tone even, and yet Sam felt a chill freeze her spine. When he turned to her, Sam felt the full impact of his eyes. The width of the room had not deceived her as to his emotions. For all his cool demeanor, Morgan was in a towering rage. Bending slightly over her, he caught her chin in his hand, lifted her face to his.

"Hello, darling. Have a nice flight?" His silky tone sent a shiver feathering down her arms, momentarily closed her throat. "You're a little pale, Redhead," he jibed knowingly. "Still sleepy?" Before she could answer, he brushed her lips with his, then released her and turned back to Duds. "Flying always makes Samantha sleepy, you know." One arrogantly cocked eyebrow dared Duds to admit he did.

Claude's intoned, "Dinner is served," saved Duds from committing himself and he sighed with relief. Sam rose to slip her hand around the arm Morgan angled at her.

"I thought you said you had business in Spain," Samantha murmured as they followed the other guests to Rachael's elegant dining room.

"A last-minute change in plans," Morgan replied quietly. "The meeting was switched to London."

Meeting with whom? And what where you doing in Italy? The unspoken questions lit a flame that burned away her shock at seeing him and replaced it with anger.

"And I thought you said you were driving to the ranch." The soft, silky words were murmured close to her ear as Morgan held Sam's chair for her, giving a good impression of gallant solicitude.

"A last-minute change in plans." Sam's smile was saccharine.

"Morgan, you take the head of the table," Rachael commanded pleasantly, "and, Dudley, you sit there, next to Samantha."

Sam breathed a sigh of relief. Her aunt's order to Morgan prevented his retaliation, even though the glittering glance he gave her before moving to the end of the table warned that he was not going to forget this.

To Sam's amazement most of her friends were acquainted with Morgan. *How had he met them? When?* In growing confusion she listened to the easy flow of conversation, somehow managing to remain cool as she answered questions, while at the same time avoided the black, amused eyes.

"Why aren't you eating?" Duds murmured. "Has he upset you? I mean by showing up so unexpectedly?"

"Yes," Sam answered honestly. "Duds, I don't understand this at all. Everyone seems to know him. You know him. How?"

"As far as everyone else goes, I haven't the foggiest," Duds answered slowly. "I met him in Australia several years ago. Not long after I went out there, as a matter of fact. You didn't know he has interests out there?"

"Yes, of course I knew," Sam answered quickly. "But— why didn't he tell me he knew you?"

"Possibly because he didn't know of our relationship, love." He smiled reassuringly. "I haven't seen him since your marriage and there was never a reason to mention you before." Duds paused, then laughed softly. "You and I, being the awful correspondents we are, could probably have gone through three mates before the news caught up to us."

Sam's soft laughter mingled with his. It was true, she hated to write letters and she knew Duds hated it too. Glancing up, the laughter died on her lips as her glance was caught, held by two chips of black ice. Sam felt a chill creep along her spine as Morgan lifted his wineglass in a mocking salute to her. Lifting her chin, she forced herself to meet his cold stare until he sipped at his wine, then she deliberately turned her face to Duds.

"How ever did he meet Aunt Rachael?" she asked Duds quietly. "Do you know?"

"Yes, I do. She told me he presented himself to her several months ago, while he was on a business trip here in London." He paused, then his face lightened. "And that may answer your first question. Perhaps Aunt Rachael introduced him to your friends at that time."

Sam was convinced he was right. It was exactly the sort of thing her Aunt Rachael would do. But why hadn't she told her Morgan was in London? Sam sighed, thinking, *because she wanted to surprise me.* That was also exactly the sort of thing she'd do.

The seemingly endless dinner finally did end and they moved into the drawing room. Sam, her mind still reeling from the sudden appearance of both Morgan and Duds, felt a throbbing begin at her temples that very quickly grew into a full-scale hammering. The way every female in the room fawned over Morgan upset Sam even more. *And he loves every minute of it,* Sam thought furiously.

Loving him, hating him, Sam watched as Morgan, so effortlessly, set her so-called friends' hearts and imaginations on fire. His long, lean body propped indolently against the mantelpiece, white teeth flashing in his dark-skinned handsome face, his soft, lazy drawl tickled their ears and delighted their senses. Sam could feel the sensuous aura he exuded surround her as well and in desperation she fought against it. Head pounding, she riled against the circumstances that had brought her to this moment. At the same time she wanted to scream at Morgan that he had no right to amuse himself with other women while she carried his child. The fact that he was unaware of her pregnancy did not even penetrate her inflamed consciousness.

No one in the room, not even Duds, who knew her so well, was aware of the rage tearing at her mind. With an outward coolness that was almost tangible, Sam masked the pain and anger that seethed below the surface.

Longing for nothing more then two aspirins and a bed, Sam nearly groaned her relief when the door closed on the last of the guests. Turning back into the wide hall, Sam blinked and glanced around quickly. Morgan seemed to have vanished into thin air. Duds forestalled Sam's asking her aunt where Morgan had gone.

"Come have a nightcap with me, Sam. You look like you need one."

Sam followed Rachael and Duds back into the drawing room and accepted the drink she didn't want.

"I'm driving down to the house at the weekend." Duds sipped his brandy, his eyes studying Sam closely. "Why don't you two come with me? You look exhausted, pet, a few days in the country air would put some color back into your cheeks."

"I don't know, Duds," Sam murmured. "But I don't think—"

"Samantha, will you come up here, please?"

Morgan's voice, quiet and authoritative, cut across Sam's words. She stiffened at his tone, then shrugged, well, at least she now knew where he'd disappeared to. With a cool, "Excuse me," she left the room and went up the wide stairway. The pain in her head that had eased somewhat in the last few minutes began pounding away at her temples again as she walked into her bedroom.

Morgan stood in the middle of the room clad only in very brief shorts, his evening clothes tossed carelessly onto the bed. Her hand still clutching the doorknob, breath catching painfully in her throat, she watched as he stepped into a pair of brown brushed denims, drew them up his long, muscular legs and over his slim hips. After tugging the zipper closed, he glanced up, his eyes cold and remote.

"It seems I've said this so often I feel I should have a recording made to save time," he attacked, "but, anyway, I'm flying to Spain tonight. When are *you* going home?"

145

He sounded angry and fed up. The pain in Sam's head stabbed viciously.

"My return reservation is for Monday night."

"Cancel it." Morgan's tone was as cold as his eyes. "I'll be back Saturday. You can fly home with me."

Rebellion flared hot and fierce inside Sam. Arrogant devil, whom did he think he was speaking to, his girl friend?

"I can't do that," she snapped icily. "I've just accepted an invitation from Duds to go down to the house for the weekend." The decision made, Sam vowed nothing Morgan said could make her change it.

"The house?" His tone was mild, much too mild.

"Duds's house, in Kent." Somehow she matched his tone. They could have been discussing the weather. "The house I grew up in." Black brows shot up in question. "Duds is my stepbrother, Morgan." Sam answered the silent question.

For some reason Sam couldn't begin to understand, the knowledge seemed to anger Morgan even more. His eyes narrowed; his voice took on a savage edge.

"Is that why he has this protective—proprietorial—attitude about you?"

His tone and words startled Sam. He sounded jealous. Morgan? Jealous? For one brief instant hope flared wildly inside Sam. It died as quickly. No, not Morgan. But Morgan had pride in abundance. She could hear his grating voice of weeks before. *You're my wife, Samantha, my woman. I don't share what's mine.* And that was it, in a nutshell, Sam thought, defeated. She was Morgan Wade's woman. His pride demanded she remain exclusively his woman until *he* decided to change the status quo.

Pain that far superseded the throbbing in her head ripped through Sam. She went hot, then cold. What about her pride? What had become of the cool, poised Samantha Denning who had effortlessly turned away from any hint of involvement with any man? And now this one man, this—this cowboy who had sold his name, dared to question her? Searing anger mingled with the pain.

"Duds is like a brother to me," she finally snapped. "His attitude has always been protective."

"How nice for you," Morgan drawled nastily. "You can tell him to relax his guard, find his own woman to protect." His voice lowered with menace. "You have a protector."

"That's going to keep you rather busy, isn't it?" Green eyes cool, Sam faced him unflinchingly. At the question in his eyes, she smiled, purred. "I hear you have a friend."

"I have many friends." His glittering black eyes held hers evenly.

"I mean a special lady friend." A flash of irritation surged through her as his lips twitched in amusement. The beast, it had taken every ounce of composure she possessed to say that calmly and he thought she was funny.

"Samantha," he drawled, "if you want to know if I've taken a mistress, why the hell don't you ask me, instead of pussyfooting around?"

Sam's stomach lurched sickeningly. Suddenly afraid, not wanting to hear him admit it, she shrugged, turned to leave the room. Closing her eyes, she lied through her teeth. "I really couldn't care less. I'm going to spend the weekend in the country. Have fun, Morgan, *wherever* you're going."

"Samantha."

Sam's hand froze in the act of turning the knob; his deadly calm tone causing her blood to run cold. She hadn't heard him move, yet his warm breath fluttered over her hair. Her breath caught in her throat when his arm slid around her waist and drew her back against his hard body. His voice, soft and caressing, made his actual words more terrifying. "If I find out he as much as touches you, I'll kill him, pseudo-brother or not."

A picture of Duds's strong face, cold and still, robbed forever of its happy grin, rose in Sam's mind. *Dear God, he means it,* she thought sickly. A shudder passed through her too-slender body and, as if he could read her mind, Morgan underlined, "I mean it, Samantha. So be a very good girl while you're enjoying the country air and I'll expect you at the ranch within two weeks. Now get out of here so I can finish dressing."

Sam fled, first the room and two days later, the city. Her weekend in the country was not altogether successful.

Duds tried repeatedly to draw her out of the self-protective shell she'd built around herself. Again and again, obviously growing more frustrated each time, he begged her to open up. He began his assault on her defenses the afternoon they arrived at the house. Rachael had retired to her room to rest before dinner while Sam and Duds strolled through the house, reacquainting themselves with the familar objects.

"Hullo! Look at this, Sam."

They were in the playroom, so named because both Sam and Duds had disparaged the word *nursery.* Sam was perched on the broad windowsill, a sad smile on her lips, paging through a much read, dogeared book of fairy tales. Glancing up at Duds's quiet exclamation, the smile softened reminicently. Her smile was reflected on Duds's plain face as he gazed down on a scruffy rag doll.

"Carmen!"

At Sam's whispered cry he lifted his eyes to hers, his eyes growing as impish as on the day they'd christened the doll.

"Ridiculous name for such a ratty-looking thing," he teased, tossing the doll to her.

Sam caught the doll, clutched it possessively against her breasts. "But that's exactly why we gave her such an exotic name, because she was so ratty." Sam's eyes clouded over mistily. "Don't you remember, Duds?"

"Yes, love, I remember."

As he walked across the room to her, his face set in somber lines. When he stopped before her, one hand came up to smooth away a stray hair that lay over her cheek.

"Sam, my pet, you worry me." Duds's voice was low, heavily edged with concern. "You're looking almost as ratty as that doll. God, if he's hurt you—" He sighed. "Can't you tell me what the trouble is?"

"Oh, Duds, it's so good to be with you again." Sam's eyes grew wistful. "I hadn't realized how much I'd missed you until I saw you again."

"Sam, my love," he chided. "You are avoiding the question."

"I know." Sam's attempt at a laugh fell flat. "I'm a big girl now, Duds. I must solve my own problems." Jumping up, she walked quickly to the door. "Come along, big brother, we haven't seen half the house yet and Aunt Rachael will be expecting her dinner soon."

After dinner Duds declared they all needed a walk in the garden. Aunt Rachael declined, but insisted Sam join him. Even though Sam knew what was coming, she went along with him.

"Look, darling, I don't want to be a nag," Duds began the minute they'd started along the path to the rose garden. "But I can see Aunt Rachael is nearly frantic about the way you've changed. Let us help you."

"Stop badgering me, Duds," Sam scolded. "If I thought there was anything either of you could do—" She stopped,

Morgan's words clear in her mind. *I'll kill him, I mean it.* Sam shook her head. "But there isn't any way you can help me."

Sam slept very little that night, tossing and turning in the canopied bed that had been hers until she was seventeen. She longed for Morgan's wide bed beneath her, and Morgan's slim frame beside her. Duds's large, beautiful house was no longer home. Even the memories of her happy childhood here seemed hazy and unreal. With a sigh of regret Sam faced the fact that there was only one place on earth that she would ever feel at home in. And that was beside Morgan, no matter where he was. And that was the one place there was no real welcome for her.

During the following two days she spent long hours in the saddle, sedately, because of her condition, following the routes she'd ridden hundreds of times as a young girl. But now the countryside she'd so loved passed by unseen. Her mind's eye, filled with the memory of a long, lean body, along with glittering black eyes and a hard, sensuous mouth, was closed to the scenery around her.

Sam managed to avoid being alone with Duds again until Sunday evening. After dinner they went into the sitting room where a cheery fire crackled invitingly. Duds kept them entertained with stories of his life in Australia and informed them he'd be going back within the month.

"I don't know quite how it happened or when," he said softly, a faraway look in his eyes. "But suddenly I knew that I wanted to spend the rest of my life there." Then to the amazement of Sam and Rachael, he added, "I'm going to sell this house. That's one of the reasons for my being here now."

It was not yet eleven when Rachael stood up and said she was going to bed. Sam, curled up in the large chair that had been her stepfather's favorite, slid her legs to the floor

150

with the intention of following her. Duds's hand on her arm stopped her.

"Samantha, are you pregnant?" he asked bluntly as soon as Rachael was out of hearing.

"What gave you that idea?" Sam hedged.

"Aunt Rachael." Duds eyed her seriously. "She's been observing you closely, as I'm sure you're aware of, and she told me this afternoon that she's convinced you are."

Sam's eyes shifted to the dying flames in the fireplace. For a few seconds she was tempted to lie, tell Duds her aunt was wrong. Sighing deeply, she shrugged her shoulders lightly. What was the point in denying it? Her answer whispered through stiff lips.

"Yes."

She heard an echo of her sigh, then a muttered curse. "That bastard."

"Duds, please." Sam's eyes swung back to his pleadingly.

"But how dare he treat you like this?" Sam had to bite back the words that Morgan dared almost anything. "Why isn't he with you now?" Duds's tone held indignant fury. "He must see how frail you look."

"He doesn't care," Sam choked.

"What the bloody hell do you mean, he doesn't care?" Duds exploded. "He doesn't care about you? He doesn't care about his child? What?"

"He doesn't care about me," Sam whispered. "And he doesn't know about the child."

"Doesn't know?" Duds repeated blankly, then, decisively, "Don't tell him."

"What? But I have to tell—"

"No." He cut in firmly. "You do not have to tell him anything." He grasped her hands, held them tightly. "Divorce him—marry me."

"Duds!" Sam's eyes flew wide in surprise. "What are you talking about? You don't love me—at least not that way."

"No, not that way," he admitted. "But I do love you and I can't go back to Australia with you looking like this. Your eyes would haunt me." His fingers squeezed hers painfully. "Love, come with me. Let me take care of you. You and your child."

"No, Duds," Sam shook her head. "Morgan would—" She was about to say Morgan would come after them, would very likely carry out his threat. Duds's angry words cut across hers.

"Morgan would deserve to lose his child, his actions convince me of that." He frowned. "You know, I liked him. From the first day I met him, I liked him. Liked and respected." He frowned again, then shrugged. "Strange, my first impressions of people are usually correct." Again he shrugged, more strongly this time. "No matter. The hell with Wade. Come with me, Sam. I promise I'll take as much care with your baby as I did with you."

"I'm sure you would." Rising swiftly, Sam lifted her hand to caress his beloved face. "But I can't let you." When he would have protested, she slid her fingers over his lips. "Sweet, sweet Duds. Somewhere, either out in the outback or wherever, there is someone for you. You'll never find her with me and Morgan's offspring hanging around your neck. Besides, he does really have a right to know about his child. I must go back and tell him."

"And if he still doesn't care," Duds groaned around her fingers. "If he doesn't even want it. Then what? What will you do?"

"I don't know," Sam confessed tiredly. "But I can always stay with Mary. She's been very kind to me, Duds. Kinder than you'll ever know."

Not for anything would Sam ever tell Duds or her aunt the reason Morgan married her. Or Mary's offer of support on hearing the terms of her father's will.

"Sam, please." Duds's voice held real pain. "Won't you reconsider? I tell you I can't go back and leave you like this."

"Yes, darling, you can," Sam insisted. "You must. I will be all right. With or without Morgan I will be all right."

Sam only wished she felt as much conviction as her forced tone implied. Later, as she undressed for bed, she stared blankly at her trembling hands. Would it ever end? She thought despairingly. Or would the pain of loving him go on and on until all thought ceased?

Their return to London on Monday morning was made in strained silence. Rachael and Duds insisted on seeing her off and when, finally, Sam boarded the big jet, she did so with a feeling of anticlimax. What awaited her at the end of her flight? Sam was afraid even to face the question, let alone try to answer it.

CHAPTER 9

Sam's drive cross-country took much longer than it should have. She stopped to stroll around whenever a city or small town appealed to her. Although it was mid-November and much of the fall foliage was gone, there were still spots where the blaze of color was breathtaking. She wandered through big stores and small shops and even bought a few pieces of heavier clothing, for the nip that had been in the air a week ago was now more of a bite. She told herself she would be a fool not to take advantage of this opportunity to see something of the country. For although she had spent a good deal of her time traveling, it had been mainly in other countries and she'd seen very little of the States. She also knew she was lying to herself. She was putting off, to the last possible minute, her meeting with Morgan.

She longed to see him and yet she was afraid. So afraid, in fact, that she had almost decided not to go at all. She was not sure she could bear to hear the words "I want a divorce."

It hadn't been an easy decision. After returning to Long Island she told herself she must think it out calmly and unemotionally, and she had. For two days she thought of nothing else. She had decided she'd divorce Morgan, stay where she was loved, have and raise her baby alone. Mary would help her. She had found herself thirty minutes later frantically packing a suitcase, asking Mary to have everything she owned shipped to the ranch, saying hasty good-byes to everyone, and jumping into the Stingray telling herself grimly she was going home, whether Morgan liked it or not.

All the way across country she had argued with herself. Did she have the right to use their child and her money to hold on to a man who didn't want her? But then, Morgan had told, no, ordered, her to return to the ranch, and didn't he have the right to at least know about his child, have that child born in his own home?

She arrived at the ranch mid-morning over a week after leaving Long Island. She was tired and stiff and mentally exhausted, but Sara's warm welcome helped chase some of the weariness. There was no sign of Morgan and Sam wondered if he had returned from Spain, only to leave again for someplace else.

She called Mary to let her know she had arrived safely, and then decided to call Babs. At the sound of Sam's voice Babs cried, "Sam, darling, when did you get back?" Her voice warm with affection, Sam answered, "Not much more than an hour ago. How is Benjie?"

Babs and Ben had not been able to go East for Deb's wedding, as Benjie had become ill. Now Babs laughed. "Oh! The imp's bouncing around like a kangaroo again. It turned out to be only a mild throat infection, but Sam, I just couldn't leave him."

"Of course not. How is everyone else?"

"Perfect," Babs enthused. "I'm so glad you got home in time for the party, Sam."

"What party?"

Babs's voice held a touch of exasperation. "That Morgan, didn't he leave you a message or anything?"

"Well, I don't think he knew just when I'd get here." Sam hedged. "I didn't know myself. Have you talked to Morgan?"

"Talked to him," Babs exclaimed. "He's here. Or, that is, he was here and he'll be back. He drove to Vegas to pick up a friend of ours, but he'll be back later today."

"I see," Sam said quietly.

"When are you coming down?" Babs's voice had an odd note now.

"I don't think—" Sam began.

"Well I do," Babs said firmly, then her voice grew urgent. "Sam, I think you'd better go throw a change of clothes, a nightie, and a dinner dress into a bag, get in your car, and come down here."

"Babs."

"I mean it, Sam. I'll look for you in a few hours. Bye now." Before Sam could say another word, Babs hung up.

Oh, what now? Sam thought. *And when did Morgan get back from Spain?* Deciding to find out, she went into the kitchen and asked point blank, "Sara, when did Mr. Morgan get back?"

"Why, over a week ago, Mrs. Sam," Sara answered. "He left again yesterday morning. He didn't say where he was going, never does, but he did say he'd call and let me know when he was coming home."

"He's at the Carters," Sam told her. "And I'll be leaving in a few minutes to join him, so please don't bother about lunch. And we will call and let you know when we'll be home." Without waiting for any questions from Sara, she left the kitchen and not much later, the house.

It was mid-afternoon when Sam pulled into the Carters' driveway. She was pulling her bag from the back of her car when Babs ran to meet her. "I'm glad you came," Babs panted. "I'm going to take you right to your room so we

156

can talk." With those words Sam found herself hurried through the house to the room she had slept in eight months before.

As Sam removed her jacket, she forced a light laugh into her voice. "Now then, pet, what's the mystery?" But she grew still at the look of concern on Babs's face and her exclaimed, "Sam, are you ill? You're so thin."

"No, of course I'm not ill," Sam was quick to assure her.

"But what is it then? Something's wrong with you. Is it Morgan?" At the look on Sam's face she added, "You love him, don't you?"

"Desperately," Sam whispered, then sank tiredly onto the bed.

"But I don't understand. What's the problem?" Babs demanded.

Sam sighed, maybe it would help to talk to someone and who better than Babs? "It's very simple, pet, he doesn't love me. In fact, he can hardly bear the sight of me."

"That I don't believe," Babs snorted. "And as for him not loving you, don't you think if you had a, well, a more normal relationship?"

"You mean, if I slept with him?" Sam asked softly.

"Well—yes."

"Oh, Babs, I've slept with him since two weeks after we were married. You know him. Can you imagine him having it any other way?"

Babs laughed ruefully. "No, as a matter of fact I can't. He's quite a man."

"Yes." It was a simple statement.

"And it still didn't jell?"

Sam shook her head briefly and Babs went on. "I don't understand it. I always thought you two were perfect for each other." Sam looked at her sharply and Babs

157

shrugged. "All right, I admit it, I've been trying to get you two together for years. I could have cried when Morgan couldn't get here for the wedding. I had it all planned. Then when you told me about your father's will, oh, Sam, I never dreamed you'd be hurt like this."

"Well, it's no good crying over it now and besides which you haven't heard the worst yet." Sam hesitated just a moment. "I'm pregnant, Babs."

"And he's still cold to you?" Babs was incredulous. "Why Sam, Morgan loves kids."

"He doesn't know," Sam said quietly.

"Well, you must tell him at once," Babs replied sharply. Her voice hardening, Babs added, "That should take care of her highness."

"Her highness?" Sam asked blankly.

"Stacy Kemper," Babs offered. "That's how I always think of her—the mercenary bitch." She laughed at Sam's startled look. "I know that's not like me. But with this one, I really mean it. She's the reason I insisted you come down. She's also the reason Morgan drove to Vegas."

Sam's eyebrows went up in question, even though she wasn't quite sure she wanted to hear any more. "As you know," Babs explained, "we've all known each other forever. Well, Stacy was one of the group, and for a while there it looked as if she really had her hooks into Morgan. That is until it became apparent that Morgan intended putting everything back into the ranch and not on her back. She took off with and married the first man with money that asked her, without bothering to say a word to Morgan. All of a sudden she was gone. We heard about her marriage later from her very embarrassed parents. I don't know how deeply it affected Morgan, for as you know, he doesn't let anything show."

Sam nodded, but remained quiet, waiting. Babs lit a

cigarette, drew deeply, then went on. "We heard a few years later that she had divorced her husband and taken up with an Italian shoe merchant or some such and then, last night, out of the blue, she phones me and invites herself here for a visit. She said she'd heard we were having a party tomorrow night and that she'd love to come. Believe it or not, Sam, I was speechless for a minute. Well, what could I say? So, of course, I said we'd be glad to have her. Then she said ever so sweetly that as she was without transportation at the moment, could someone come to Vegas for her? And as Ben had to be away most of today on business, Morgan offered to go. And I don't like it, Sam, I don't like it at all." Babs sat back, punched out her cigarette, and immediately lit another.

Sam didn't like it either, although she said nothing. She lit a cigarette and sat thinking as she studied the glowing red tip. An Italian shoe merchant—and Morgan had been seen with a woman in Italy. A coincidence? It was hardly likely. Had he brought this woman, this Stacy, back with him? That seemed much more likely. Yet he had told her to come back to the ranch. What sort of game was he playing? First Carolyn, now this Stacy person. *Damn him, damn him, damn him,* Sam's mind cried furiously. Should she leave? Not wait to suffer the humiliation of being introduced to his ex, and now current, lover? Babs made the decision for her as, jumping to her feet, she picked up Sam's jacket and bag and said firmly, "Come with me." She flung the door open and marched across the hall, to fling another door open and drop Sam's things onto the bed.

Sam glanced around as she entered the room and stopped dead. Morgan's suitcase lay on a bench at the foot of the bed; his brush and comb rested on the dresser.

"Really, Babs," she began, only to be cut off by a very determined-sounding Babs.

"Honey, I don't know how Morgan feels about you. I don't know if he feels anything for her. Hell, I don't know how he feels about much of anything, the clam. But in my house husbands and wives sleep together, not husbands and friends." At the look of pain on Sam's face she added with force, "Oh, Sam, at least make a fight of it. Don't run away."

Sam stayed.

She spent the rest of the afternoon getting reacquainted with Benjie and an amazingly bigger Mark. Ben got home just in time for dinner. Morgan didn't. Ben seemed genuinely happy to see Sam and kept the conversation going throughout the meal.

A few hours later Sam sat curled into a chair in the living room. She had stopped speaking to sip sherry, and had opened her mouth to continue her description of Deb and Bryan's wedding for Babs and Ben, when she went rigid.

Babs glanced swiftly at Ben and then at Sam. They had all heard the sound of the Jaguar as it came up the drive.

Sam was well aware that Babs had filled Ben in on the situation, and she had a moment of pure panic. *I shouldn't be here,* she thought. They had all been friends in one way or other and the last thing Sam wanted in the world was to bring dissension of any kind into this obviously happy home. Before she could unfreeze herself enough to move, the door opened and Morgan strode into the room followed by a woman a few years younger than himself.

Sam barely looked at the woman, for her eyes fastened on Morgan. The night was cold and he was dressed in a heavy tan sheepskin-lined jacket, collar up. Along with black leather driving gloves, boots, and the inevitable black Andalusian hat, he looked rugged and knee-weakeningly masculine. On seeing Sam he stopped in his tracks and she thought she saw an odd look on his face, but it was gone in an instant. He reached up to pull his hat off, his face expressionless, as he moved into the room, closer to her. She was glad she was sitting down, for there was no mistaking the look in those black eyes. He was angry, very angry. As he shrugged out of his jacket, he said in a voice even and smooth as silk, "Well, Samantha, when did you get home? And how did you get here?"

Sam hated when his voice took on that silky tone. Lifting her chin, she answered coolly, "I got home this morning and I drove here in my own car. It's parked in the garage. And I'm fine, thank you," she tacked on, reminding him he hadn't asked. Very slowly she turned her head to look pointedly and haughtily at the woman who had walked up to stand beside him.

She saw the corner of his mouth twitch. In what? Amusement? Annoyance? She was too busy studying the woman to figure out which. She was, without doubt, beautiful. Hair and brows as black as Morgan's with startling red lips in a perfect matte white face. Her eyes a blue so pale as to be almost colorless. But she had, Sam thought, the look of—what? The word *predator* jumped into Sam's mind.

Morgan's smooth voice drew her attention. "Samantha, this is Stacy Kemper, an old friend. Stacy, my wife."

"Hello, Samantha." Stacy's teeth flashed white. Her voice was pure honey.

Sam did not rise or extend her hand. With only a hint of a smile touching her lips, she nodded slightly and murmured frostily, "Miss Kemper."

In a capsulized instant Sam's cool, green eyes recorded the reaction of the other four. Ben's face revealed his surprise. Babs seemed to be having a great deal of trouble keeping a straight face. Stacy withdrew her hand slowly, a look of wariness in the pale blue eyes. And Morgan? Morgan's reaction baffled her. Although he had stiffened at her arrogant iciness, his black eyes, locked on hers, glittered with an emotion she couldn't quite define. He was either extremely amused or flat-out furious. But which? Sam had a sudden overwhelming urge to run for her life. Sheer will power kept her motionless in her seat, her eyes steady on his.

After what seemed half a lifetime, but was actually only seconds, Morgan released his visual hammerlock. Turning away with a casual ease that mocked the tension his eyes had generated so easily in Sam, Morgan tossed his jacket and Stacy's coat onto a chair and grinned at Ben and Babs.

"Stacy informed me, not ten minutes ago, that she was dying for a drink." His lazy drawl shattered the stillness that had held them all motionless and galvanized Babs into action.

"Of course," she exclaimed, jumping to her feet. "What a rotten hostess I am. Ben, will you get the drinks while I hang up their coats?" As if she realized she was speaking much too fast, Babs stood stock still, looked directly at Stacy, and said slowly and distinctly, "It's been a long time, Stacy. How are you?"

Studying Stacy with an outward composure that required every ounce of will power she possessed, Sam didn't even hear her response to Babs or, for that matter, any of the ensuing conversation until a laughing remark from Stacy penetrated her concentration.

"I suddenly just could not win." The malicious gleam of satisfaction in her pale-blue eyes contradicted the rueful pout on her lush red mouth. "The dice had gone absolutely stone cold for me." Calculating eyes flickered over Sam

162

and the rueful pout smoothed into a smug smile. "If Morgan hadn't been there to cover my losses, well, I just don't know what I'd done."

Blind fury turned Sam's eyes into chips of green ice. Whose money had he used to cover Stacy's losses with? And how had she repaid him? By allowing him to cover her as well? The questions stabbed painfully at Sam's mind and the green ice chips swung to Morgan in accusation.

One black brow arched elegantly; he returned her stare blandly, lips twitching tauntingly.

Fed up, sick to her stomach, Sam finished her drink, placed the glass carefully on the coaster on the table at her elbow and, rising with unconscious grace, excused herself and left the room. Morgan did not follow her.

She just made it to the bathroom. After her stomach had relieved itself of her dinner and the sherry she'd gulped, she cleaned her face, brushed her teeth, then stood irresolutely in the middle of the bedroom, Morgan's bedroom, wondering what to do. Surely, she finally decided, Morgan had not entertained the idea of having Stacy warm his bed while he was in his best friend's home? With a shrug she slipped between the sheets. Her last conscious thought was, what would he think when he found his wife in his bed?

Sam was not to know, for she fell into a deep, exhausted sleep. She half awoke during the night, feeling chilly, and without thinking burrowed under the covers closer to the warm body beside her. She was only vaguely, if pleasantly, aware of a feeling of warmth as Morgan's arms slid around her, drew her even closer against him. She didn't remember it in the morning, but she knew he had slept beside her, as his pillow still held the impression from his head. And she sadly decided she'd dreamed the sound of his voice, almost a groan, in the night, whispering her name.

163

Stacy had not yet put in an appearance, Ben had finished eating and left the table, and Sam and Babs were sipping their second cups of coffee and discussing the new fall clothes, when Morgan walked lazily into the dining room. He poured himself coffee, reached across the table to pick up a piece of bacon Sam had not eaten from her plate, cocked a brow at her, and drawled sardonically, "And how did you leave your—ah—friends, Samantha?"

Sam decided she disliked this sardonic tone as much as his silky one. Looking at him coldly, she answered in kind, "With much difficulty, I assure you." Rising slowly, she turned her back to him and left the room thinking, *and so the battle is joined—again.* The next day passed smoothly enough as Sam saw little of Morgan or Stacy.

Sam was left alone to dress for the evening, as Morgan had finished dressing and left the room while she made up her face in the bathroom. She had brought with her a gown she had bought, with the coming holidays in mind, on her drive West. After slipping the gown on, she carefully brushed her hair, then, stepping back, viewed the results critically. The gown, of deep-green velvet, was simply cut, with close-fitting long sleeves and bodice snug to her still small waist. The neckline plunged in a V to a point between her breasts. The full skirt came to an inch above the floor. She went over to the dresser, removed the black case, flipped the lid, picked out the emerald ring she'd removed before starting her trip, and slid it onto her finger. Then she lifted out the pendant and fastened the chain around her neck. The emerald, which rested just below the base of her throat, glowing warm and rich against her now pale gold skin, seemed to reflect the exact color of her eyes and the circle of diamonds glinted with light. Giving a quick nod of satisfaction, she left the room.

She intercepted Babs in the hallway between the dining and living rooms.

"Good grief, Sam," Babs, wide eyes fastened on the emerald pendant, whispered in an awed tone. "That's the most fantastically beautiful thing I've ever seen. Did you knock over Cartier's or something?"

"That's just the half of it, pet." Laughing softly, Sam held out her hand, moved it slightly so the light got caught in the large stone on her finger.

"Wherever did you get them?" Babs breathed hoarsely.

"The ring was a birthday present," Sam replied reluctantly. "The pendant was a belated wedding gift."

"Who from, for heaven's sake?" Babs dragged her eyes from the ring, lifted them to Sam's face, and added. "An oil-rich Arab sheikh?"

"I don't know any Arab sheikh, oil rich or otherwise," Sam murmured. She hesitated then said even more softly, "The gifts were from Morgan."

"And you, my dear peabrain, claim he doesn't care for you?" Babs's already wide eyes widened even more. "Don't you know only a man in love with his wife will buy jewelry like that for her?"

All that long evening Sam clung to Babs's words, determinedly pushing away the thought that the gems were purchased with her money.

Entering the living room, Sam came to a stop at the barrage of greetings called to her by the dozen people gathered there. Stacy, beautiful in an ice-blue sheath that gave her a deceptively fragile look, stood watchfully by the liquor cabinet, but there was no sign of Morgan. Babs laughingly joined Ben as the cry went up for a belated wedding toast and, as they refilled glasses, Sam fought a rising unease. Where was Morgan?

"We can't have a toast without the bridegroom." The

protest was registered by a tiny brunette whose name escaped Sam at the moment. "Where is Morgan, anyway?"

"Right here, Karen."

The lazy drawl, so close behind her, sent a shiver down Sam's spine. The hand that curved around her waist drew her close to his side, turning the shiver to a tongue of fire.

The toast was given, then Sam felt his fingers tighten against her side as Karen chided, "Well, for heaven's sake, Morgan, kiss the bride."

Startled, Sam glanced at him quickly, saw the devil dance in his eyes as he lowered his head to hers. His lips touched hers briefly and yet even in that fleeting instant he reasserted his ownership. With a muffled gasp of shock, Sam felt the tip of his tongue, hard as the tip of a stiletto, pierce her unwilling mouth. Her eyes shot angry green sparks at him when he lifted his head, murmuring tauntingly, "Do you still feel like a bride, Sam?"

In retaliation she let out the first thing that came into her mind. "A somewhat battered one, perhaps."

Though his facial expression didn't change, Morgan's body stiffened and his eyes turned cold and hard. His voice dropped even lower than before, and held a frightening edge of menace.

"Touché, Redhead."

Hating herself, hating him, Sam watched in amazement as his eyes went flat before he turned back to the guests, a deceptively relaxed smile on his face. Drawing her with him, he sauntered into the room, his tone languid as he responded to the renewed calls of congratulations.

When the well-wishing was finally over, the punishing hold on Sam's waist was removed and Morgan left her side. Moving casually, as though his only interest lay in refilling his glass, he joined a pouting Stacy, still standing sentinel by the liquor cabinet.

At any other time Sam would have enjoyed the party. Babs, Ben, and Morgan's friends accepted her as one of their own. They had known previously of the closeness between Sam and Babs, and the fact that she was now Morgan's wife seemed to delight them. The conversation was easy, most times amusing. The food was delicious. Sam was miserable. Although Morgan was careful not to be too blatantly attentive to Stacy, the smug, self-satisfied expression her beautiful face wore dashed all the secret hopes Sam had harbored in her heart as she'd driven West. She kept up with the chatter and badinage until shortly after three and then, unable to bear any more, she excused herself and went to her room.

Within minutes she was crawling into bed, tormenting herself with the question of whether Morgan would spend what was left of the night in their room or Stacy's. But at least the torment was short-lived, for as the night before, she was asleep as soon as her head touched down on her pillow.

CHAPTER 10

The sound of Morgan's voice nudged her awake. Forcing her eyes open, she dully registered two facts. He was fully dressed and was holding a steaming mug of coffee in his hand. He watched her silently as she sat up and rested her back against the headboard.

"I'm going home this morning, are you going with me?" His voice was flat and even as he handed her the mug.

Sam sipped gingerly at the hot brew before answering. "Yes." His next words turned her insides to ice.

"Good. We have some talking to do, Samantha, and I'd prefer to do it in private."

She gulped her coffee too quickly, the hot liquid making her cough and, reaching out swiftly, he plucked the mug from her hands. Watching her, he drank from the mug, then handed it back after she'd caught her breath, wiping her eyes with the back of her hand. "I can't actually go with you, I have my car."

"I remember." His voice held the tone of a parent talking to a dim-witted child. "I'll follow you in the Jag."

"All right. What time do you want to leave?"

She emptied the cup and he took it from her. "More?" She nodded as glancing at his watch he told her, "It's eight thirty. I'd like to be ready to go in an hour. Marie's getting breakfast now."

Sam's voice was startled. "But we can't leave without seeing Babs and Ben."

"I have no intention of doing so," he replied patiently. "But they'll probably be up by then. Now you'd better get moving. I'll get your coffee." He walked to the door and stopped, hand on the knob, when Sam said, "Morgan, I told Sara we'd call."

"I called her last night," he answered without turning. "And told her to stay home today, take the day off, as we wanted to be alone." He opened the door and went through, closing it softly behind him.

Had his voice been mocking? she asked herself, pulling her nightgown over her head as she leaped from the bed. Deciding it was, she grabbed panty hose and bra from the dresser drawer and dashed into the bathroom and under the shower.

She walked back into the bedroom ten minutes later to find Morgan sitting in the chair by the window sipping her fresh coffee. She felt suddenly shy of him seeing her in nothing but panty hose and bra and turning away quickly stepped into jeans and pulled a bulky knit sweater over her head. When she turned around to face him, he handed her the mug with a twisted smile. "Breakfast is just about ready, you'd better pack." He placed her bag on the bench at the foot of the bed and flipped the lid open as Sam collected her makeup and toiletries from the bathroom. She packed the few things she'd brought with her quickly and, as she was carefully folding her gown, Morgan said softly, "That's a lovely dress, Samantha, it suits you."

Sam stood still in shocked speechlessness a moment before answering, her voice sounding wooden to her own ears, "Thank you, I think that's everything." But she stole a glance at him as she closed the lid and was surprised to see the bleak look was quickly gone from his face.

169

He got her jacket and picked up her suitcase, then stood waiting at the door while she put on her boots.

As Sam left the room, she heard voices from the nursery. Telling Morgan she'd join him in a few minutes, she went in to say good-bye to the boys. She talked a few minutes with Judy, then, with a tug at her heart, gave good-bye hugs and kisses to Benjie and Mark. She left the nursery quickly and walked down the hall to the dining room noticing her suitcase sitting next to Morgan's at the front door.

Morgan was filling two plates from the covered dishes on the sideboard, so she slipped into her chair and sipped her juice. When he placed her plate in front of her she bit back the protest that rose to her lips. How in the world would she eat all that food? she thought, eyeing him warily. Nevertheless she tried.

He had finished, poured himself a second cup of coffee, and lit a cigarette, watching her steadily, when Babs and Ben joined them.

"I see you're all set to take off after you've eaten." Babs filled her plate and sat down saying lightly, "You weren't going without saying good-bye, were you?"

"Of course not," Sam cried.

"I'd have come in and tilted your bed," Morgan added dryly.

Ben laughed softly. "I don't doubt it a minute."

"Nor I," Babs teased, before adding seriously, "I hope it's not eight months before we see you two again. As a matter of fact, we'd like to have you for Christmas."

"Well, we'll see," Sam hedged, then nearly jumped as Babs gave her a kick under the table while turning a sweet smile on Morgan. "Do you think you could make it?"

"I don't see why not." Morgan's white teeth flashed in

a grin as he answered blandly. "Let us know what time, Babs."

"I will," came the emphatic reply.

They waited until Babs and Ben had finished eating, then made their way out. As Morgan stashed their suitcases and Ben brought Sam's car from the garage, Babs whispered, "Have you told him?" Sam shook her head. "Well, do it as soon as you get home," Babs ordered. Sam hugged Babs, whispered, "I will and thanks for being my friend." Babs kissed Sam lightly on the cheek. "Always, you know that, Sam."

Sam, feeling tears too close, nodded and slid behind the wheel. Giving a quick wave, she drove out of the driveway, the Jaguar right behind her. Halfway to the ranch Sam began to resent the short distance Morgan kept between them. *As if I can't be trusted behind the wheel,* she thought peevishly, her foot pushing the pedal to the floor. The Stingray shot ahead and in no time had put some distance between them. Her satisfaction was short-lived, however, as glancing in the rearview mirror, she saw the Jag gaining rapidly on her. *I should have known better,* she was thinking when the car hit an oil slick and went into a spin. Sam gripped the wheel, but going with the spin, not trying to halt it, and by some quirk of fate, the car didn't roll over. She finally managed to bring it to a stop facing in the same direction she'd been going. She was still clutching the wheel, shaking all over, when the door was flung open. "What kind of a stupid trick was that?" It was the closest thing to a shout she'd ever heard from Morgan. "You crazy broad, are you trying to kill yourself?"

It was the wrong side of enough. Sam refused to listen to this cowboy speak to her like this any longer. The engine was still idling, and forcing her shaking fingers from the wheel, Sam did two things at once. She reached

171

out for the handle and slammed the door shut, seeing Morgan straighten in surprise as she did so, then she floored the pedal again. She kept it floored until she reached the road to the ranch property, thankful of the sparse traffic, and then only slowed down a fraction until reaching their driveway. She crawled along the driveway sedately, parked in front of the garage, jumped from the car, and ran to the back door of the house, rummaging in her bag for the kitchen door key.

Inside the kitchen she stood breathing deeply, shaking all over with reaction. Her body jerked when she heard the Jag purr to a stop in the drive and she ran from the room through the house to the bedroom. She flung her jacket and purse onto a chair and sat on the side of the bed fighting for control. *I must leave him, get away from here,* she was thinking wildly when he walked into the room in a cold fury. Wincing at the slam of the door, she repeated her thought aloud, "I'm going to leave you, Morgan, get a divorce."

His eyes glittered like two pieces of wet coal and his voice was icy.

"What kind of games are you playing? What the hell did you come back for?"

At the end of her rope, her voice rose. "I'm not playing games."

"No?" Morgan's eyes narrowed as he walked slowly toward her. "You didn't drive all the way out here just to see the scenery. Or to tell me you were going to divorce me. So let's have it."

"It doesn't matter." Sam had to fight to keep her voice even.

"What doesn't matter?" He stopped in front of her. "What aren't you telling me?" At Sam's helpless shrug his tone lowered threateningly. "Tell me, Samantha."

172

"I'm pregnant," Sam whispered starkly.

Cold eyes in a rock-hard face raked over her. "Is it mine?"

"Oh, God," Sam's whisper held pain, anguish. "Oh, *God.*" Feeling nausea churn upward from her stomach to her throat, Sam brought one hand up to cover her mouth, moved to get up, away from his cold eyes. His hand grasped her shoulder, held her still as he sat down beside her.

"I'm sorry," Morgan grated harshly. "I had to know. When?"

"What?"

"When is the baby due?" he snapped.

"Late spring," Sam whispered. "The end of May."

"I see." He had finished his mental calculations; his deductions were only partly correct. "And you drove all the way out here just to watch my face when you told me?"

Sam's eyes widened. He really believed she'd come to lay some sort of guilt trip on him, torment him, because of his actions on the night she'd conceived. His opinion of her hurt unbearably. Blinking quickly against the hot sting in her eyes, Sam looked up at him. His face was set in hard, rigid lines; his eyes studied her coldly.

"You really hate me," she whispered brokenly, "don't you, Morgan?"

The hand gripping her shoulder tightened painfully while his other hand grasped the hair at the back of her head and forced her face close to his.

"Hate you?" he grated. "You redheaded witch, I love you."

His crushing mouth smothered her gasp of disbelief. Had he really said he loved her? Wild hope mingled with

173

the fire surging through her veins. The smothered gasp came out as a low moan when he lifted his head.

"Morgan."

"No." His lips teased hers. "Don't talk. You can add my scalp to all the others on your belt," he groaned against her mouth. "But don't talk. Not now. It's been so long, Sam."

In between deep, hungry kisses their clothes were abandoned and then, as their hunger grew urgent, it was the two of them that gave in to their abandon. Driven to the edge of delirium by his hands, his mouth, Sam clung to Morgan, moaning softly deep in her throat, begging him to make her a part of him.

He came to her almost hesitantly, but that hesitancy was soon lost to the need to possess and be possessed. As their shudders subsided to gentle tremors, Sam's hand lightly caressed Morgan's warm, moist back.

"Don't go, Sam." The words were muffled against her hair. "These last weeks have been hell. The idea of spending the rest of my life without you is unbearable. Stay with me. Bargain with me one more time."

"Bargain?"

Morgan sighed, then the sweet weight of his body left hers and he lay beside her, his fingers lacing through hers as if he couldn't bear the thought of breaking all physical contact.

"I want my baby," Morgan said softly. "Your baby." His fingers crushed hers. "I want you. I'll match the amount that was laid on the line last March, if you'll stay with me."

"Match the amount?" Sam repeated incredulously.

"Yes," he answered flatly. "I can't give it to you in one lump sum, but I'll put one million a year, for the next five years, in an account in your name."

"But how?"

"I don't need your money, Sam. I never have," he went on in the same flat tone. "And I haven't touched it."

"But Babs said—" Sam began uncertainly, but he cut her off.

"I know what my friends think and I've let them think it. It's kept the cats away. But I was never as broke as they thought and I've made a lot of money over the last ten years. I'm a fairly rich man, Samantha, and I worked like hell for every cent of it."

Confusion kept Sam quiet for several minutes. His tight grip on her hand was causing her ring to dig into her finger and that sparked a sudden thought.

"My jewelry and the plane and the Jag?"

"I paid for them. Your charge accounts too." His flat tone grew an edge of amusement. "That's why your lawyers wanted to see me. They couldn't understand why we hadn't drawn on the money."

"But when you bought the plane and the car you consulted me!" Sam exclaimed.

"Of course." All traces of amusement fled. "You're my wife."

"I don't understand, Morgan." Sam spoke slowly. "If you didn't need the money then why did you—"

"Marry you?" Morgan finished for her. "I wanted you," he added bluntly.

"Physically?" Sam whispered.

"Yes."

His head turned on the pillow and Sam found herself looking directly into unreadable black eyes.

"I wanted you physically," he said clearly. "From the minute I looked up and saw you framed in the doorway of Ben's living room." His eyes roamed over her face, a small fire springing to life. "I've wanted many women,

Samantha, and I had most of the ones I wanted, but I had never wanted a woman on sight as badly as I wanted you." The fire leaped a little higher in his eyes. "I had to fight the urge to tear your clothes off and throw you onto the floor."

"But you seemed to dislike me," Sam gasped, the flame in his eyes igniting a similar one inside her body.

"What I disliked was the intensity of my own feelings." His free hand came up to touch her face, his long index finger traced the outline of her upper lip. "But believe me, I'd decided there and then that I'd have you. And when Ben outlined your proposition, I agreed at once. If I hadn't fallen in love with you by the time we got married I'd have taken you a lot sooner than I did." The tip of his finger slid between her lips, brushed the edge of her teeth. "And when I did take you, it was because I could no longer control myself."

His eyes, watching the play of his finger, darkened with fresh desire. His other hand loosened, moved to caress the inside of her arm as his head moved closer to hers.

"Will you bargain one last time, Sam?" he asked huskily.

"You want to *buy* me, Morgan?" Sam murmured tremulously.

"If that's the way it must be, yes," he said bluntly. "You and our baby."

"Who was conceived in violence."

The moment the words were out, Sam wished them unsaid. Raw pain flashed in Morgan's eyes before he rolled away from her to sit up on the edge of the bed.

"Yes, who was conceived in violence," he repeated harshly, long fingers of one hand raking through his hair. Sam barely heard the whispered words that followed. "But welcomed with love."

He turned back to face her again, his hard, muscular shoulders gleaming darkly in the late afternoon sunlight slanting through the window. The golden mellow rays brought into relief the harshly defined features of his face.

"And he *will* be welcomed with love, I promise you that." His hand massaged the back of his neck and his voice grew husky again. "I've hurt you badly and I know it." He paused, his hand dropping to his side, before adding roughly, "I wanted to hurt you."

"Why, Morgan?" Sam asked softly, then wished she'd been still as she lay and watched the fire of desire explode into a blaze of fury.

"Why? Because I had been bought and paid for, that's why."

"But you just said you didn't need—"

"But you didn't know that, did you?" Morgan's harsh voice slashed across her protest. "You wore my ring and you shared my bed and then you calmly told me you'd sleep with anyone you wanted to."

"Morgan, please," Sam cried, suddenly frightened. "I never meant it. I was lashing out in jealousy."

"Jealousy?" Morgan looked completely stunned. "Jealous of whom?"

"Carolyn." At his totally blank expression, Sam cried, "I saw you with her in the garden the night of the party. I saw you take her into your arms." The anger she'd felt that night returned to jab at her. "Did you take her with you the first time you left Long Island?"

"I did not." The denial was prompt and emphatic and held the unmistakable ring of truth. "And I did not take her into my arms in the garden. She had a few suggestions along that line but I politely declined." One black brow arched sardonically. "I figured I had enough to handle

177

with a fiery-tempered, green-eyed redhead. The last thing I needed was a doll-faced, simpering blonde."

"And what about a white-faced, black-haired, ex-mistress of an Italian shoe merchant?" Sam shot back, forgetting her nakedness as she sat up to glare at him.

"What about her?" Morgan returned easily.

"Do you deny you were with her in Italy and London?" Sam almost screamed at him. "Or that you damned near crawled all over her last night?"

The light of devilment jumping into his eyes, Morgan studied her for long moments before he dropped back onto the bed, his body shaking with laughter.

Staring at him in impotent rage, Sam was struck with two conflicting urges. The first was to slap his laughing face. The second was to caress his smooth dark skin. Trembling with anger and the longing to be in his arms, Sam snapped, "Damn you, Morgan, answer me."

With the swiftness of tightly coiled springs suddenly released, Morgan's arms shot out and his hands, grasping her shoulders, hauled her down with a jarring thud on top of him.

"No, you answer me," he demanded. "Do you love me?"

"Morgan, let me go." Sam struggled wildly, gasping softly at the sensations the feel of his hair-roughened chest against her breasts sent splintering through her body.

"Do you love me?" One hard hand released her shoulder to grip the back of her head and force her lips to within a whisper of his.

"Yes." His lips touched hers briefly. "Yes." Another touch. "Oh, yes." With a sigh Sam sought the searing brand that was his mouth.

* * *

Sam surfaced to the pearl-gray of pre-dawn, reaching for Morgan before she opened her eyes. When her searching hands found nothing but empty sheets beside her, she opened her eyes, called his name unsteadily.

"Coming." The reassuring sound of his voice and the fragrant scent of freshly brewed coffee preceded him into the room.

Sam was sitting up, covers draped around her shoulders against the chill morning air, when he sauntered into the room, a mug of coffee in each hand.

"Good morning."

A light shiver rippled over Sam's shoulder at the husky timbre of his voice, the altogether male look of him. He was freshly showered and his taut, dark-skinned cheeks gleamed with an attractive, just-shaven sheen. Dressed in tight jeans and a finely knit, longsleeved white pullover, merely looking at him did crazy things to Sam's senses.

Morgan saw her shiver and, after setting the mugs down on the nightstand beside the bed, he strode to the closet that ran the length of the far wall, pulled out a white terrycloth robe, and walked back to the bed holding the robe for her as he would a coat.

Unsure of him still, Sam hesitated, but when one black brow went up slowly in a ark she drew a deep breath, scrambled off the bed, and slid her arms into the sleeves of the robe. As her trembling fingers pulled the belt tight, his hands tightened on her shoulders then were removed.

"Drink your coffee before it gets cold."

Turning quickly, Sam took the mug he held out to her then sank onto the side of the bed, her eyes fastened on his back as he walked to the window, stood staring through the glass, his face set in brooding lines.

His strangely cool, withdrawn attitude, following so swiftly on the heels of his hot, passionate lovemaking, sent

179

a shaft of fear through Sam's heart. Sipping the hot brew she watched him nervously, trying to steel herself for whatever he had to say.

"Do you still want to leave me, Samantha?" He did not turn his head to look at her and Sam shivered again, this time at the flat emotionless tone of his voice. "Do you still want a divorce?"

Sam's mouth went completely dry. Was he trying to tell her he wanted her to go? After the night they'd just spent together? She considered using delaying tactics in an effort to draw him out, find out exactly what he wanted. For herself, well, she knew what she wanted but, if he wanted his freedom, her pride dictated that she should give it to him, walk away from this debacle with her head still high. Her sigh of surrender could be heard across the room more clearly than the whispered words that followed it.

"No, I don't want to leave. I don't want a divorce." Sam drew a deep breath. "I love you, Morgan. I want to stay here with you."

She couldn't see his face, but she heard his breath expelled slowly, as if he'd been holding it a long time. Then he turned to face her, his knuckles white from gripping his coffee mug.

"About Stacy," he said quietly. "I was with her in Italy and London."

Panic crawled through Sam's mind. Had he deliberately waited for her to commit herself before telling her about Stacy? She was suddenly sure she didn't want to hear any more, but before she could tell him he asked, "Who told you, Dudley?"

"Yes."

"I see." His tone was so cold Sam shivered again.

"No, Morgan, you don't." Sam stared unflinchingly into those cold, black eyes. "What I told you in London

180

was true. Duds is like an older brother to me, nothing more. He is protective of me, he always has been. That's the only reason he told me you had been seen with her."

"I see," Morgan repeated, but in a different tone. "It seems I owe the both of you an apology for what I was thinking about your relationship." He finished his coffee and placed the mug on the wide windowsill behind him before going on calmly. "I ran into Stacy in Spain. She told me bluntly that she had had a violent argument with her shoe merchant friend and that, as he had acquired another to replace her, he was kicking her out."

"But what was she doing in Spain?" Sam asked in confusion.

"She said she was paying a last visit to some close friends," Morgan replied dryly. "When I mentioned that due to a change in business plans I was flying to London in two days, she begged me to take her with me." He shrugged carelessly. "We flew to Italy the next day. She collected some of her things and made arrangements for the rest to be sent to her parents' here in Nevada. We flew to London the following morning."

"Did you bring her with you when you came back to the States?" Sam asked hoarsely.

"Yes," he answered flatly. "I also gave her some money. In Spain, in London, and again, two days ago, in Vegas."

Sam closed her eyes against the sudden hot sting of tears, swallowed with difficulty against the dryness in her throat. The sharpness of his tone brought her eyelids up again.

"I did not touch her. Not in any personal way. I wasn't even tempted." His lips curved in self-derision. "Even if I had been, I doubt if I'd been able to do anything about it. She doesn't have red hair."

"Morgan." A different kind of shiver slid down Sam's

spine and her heart gave a wild double thump. "She seemed very sure of herself at Babs's," she said carefully. "Did you make any—promises?"

"Are you out of your beautiful red head?" Morgan grated. "I just finished telling you I can't see any other woman—" He broke off suddenly then added softly, "I wanted you to assume there was something between Stacy and me." His voice dropped to a ragged whisper. "I thought that if I couldn't get at you any other way, maybe I could hurt you through your pride." He laughed harshly in self-mockery. "You were so cool, so untouched, by it all. I was sure the only one I'd managed to hurt was myself, again."

"Again?" Sam repeated. "But when—?"

"The night of the party," Morgan answered her question before she'd finished asking it. "I was so damned mad. I've been mad ever since."

"But, I—"

"Not at you," he interrupted again. "At myself."

"Why?"

"Why?" He barked. "Good God, Sam, I'd never physically harmed a woman in my life and I'd savaged you." His lips twisted in a grim mockery of a smile. "And I'd done it deliberately. I walked into that bedroom knowing I was going to hurt you in some way."

"Morgan, stop."

His smile, the harsh lines of self-disgust that edged his face, clutched at Sam's heart. The punishment he had meted out to her was as nothing compared to the punishment he'd obviously inflicted on himself.

"You were so magnificent," Morgan went on as if he hadn't heard her. His black eyes grew warm with admiration. "You are some woman, Red, and I handled you badly." His smile turned self-derisive. "It was a new experience for me—the jealous lover. I'd never cared enough about any other woman to feel jealousy."

"Jealous?" Sam breathed, wide eyed. "You, Morgan?"

"Funny, isn't it?" Morgan shrugged, as if uncomfortable in a too snugly fitting coat. "Want to hear something even funnier? I was scared. Deep down gut scared."

"*That* I find impossible to believe."

"It's true all the same." Morgan's eyes caressed her face. "The scary feeling began soon after that first night we slept together. It got worse every time I had to go away. I was so damned scared that one day I'd come home and find you'd gone." He smiled ruefully. "Last summer when you first started to lose weight I grasped at the idea you might be pregnant."

"You wanted me to be pregnant?" Sam cried in disbelief. "But I was positive you'd be angry if I was."

Morgan's head moved sharply in the negative. "I was praying you'd become pregnant. I thought—I hoped that might keep you with me." Again that rueful smile curved his lips. "Stupid, I know. But, as I said, I was running scared and willing to grasp at any straw."

Wide-eyed, stunned, Sam stared at Morgan as if at a stranger. Where was the cold-eyed, unfeeling, arrogant man she had thought she'd married? A series of scenes flashed through her mind. Morgan, Benjie clasped firmly in his arms, laughing down at Mark. Morgan, his eyes soft, his voice gentle, asking Deb to be his sister. Morgan, his eyes filled with contrition, giving her his word that he'd never hurt her again. Suddenly she knew that if this man was a stranger to her, she had no one to blame but herself. Drawing a deep breath, Sam decided to get to know this stranger better.

"Of course"—Morgan's eyes skimmed her body possessively—"I dreaded that trip to Long Island. I felt sure that once you left the ranch you'd never come back. You'd been jetting around the world all your life." He waved his hand to indicate not only the room but the whole property. "After the world, what could this place offer you?"

"You."

All the harshness drained out of his face at her whispered reply. His eyes, flaring with rekindled passion, set off tiny explosions of pure joy all through Sam's body. She shivered deliciously as he walked slowly to her.

"I love you, Sam."

Cradling her head in his hands, he tilted her head back. As he lowered his head she chided, "You said I was your woman."

"I also said you're my wife." His lips brushed hers tantalizingly. "I want you to remain my wife. Tell me you love me, Sam."

"I love you, Morgan."

His mouth touched hers, the pressure increasing as he slid his body onto the bed. His arms, closing around her, drew her body alongside his. His mouth left hers, sought the tender skin behind her ear.

"I could bear not being your wife, Morgan."

"Samantha!"

Morgan's head jerked back and his black eyes pinned hers, narrowed at the teasing light he found there.

"But I don't think I could bear not being your woman."

Sam swam the length of the pool slowly, reveling in the delicious feel of the water on her body. It was the first time she'd been able to go into the pool and the July sun had quickly pinkened her pale skin. Pulling her body through the water, Sam was grateful for her renewed energy, the strength in her arms. For so many weeks after she'd left the hospital she'd been so damnably, stupidly weak.

Movement along the side of the pool caught her eye and she turned her head to see who it was. The sight of her husband's tall form sent all thoughts of her health out of her head. Dropping her feet to the floor of the pool, Sam watched as Morgan walked to the edge of the pool and stood, hands on hips, watching her. He was incredibly dusty and incredibly sweaty and incredibly beautiful.

"Come here, Red."

Sam was galvanized into action by the soft order. When she reached the side of the pool, she raised her hands for him to help her out. Ignoring her hands, Morgan bent down and caught her firmly under the arms and lifted her out of the water as he straightened. When she stood, dripping, in front of him, his hands dropped to circle her slender waist.

"Do you have permission to go in the water?"

Morgan's eyes, searching her face, warned her she'd better have.

"Yes," Sam replied softly, knowing full well the importance of her answer. "I gave the doctor a verbal report on my condition by phone this morning," she went on to explain. "He told me I could resume swimming and all normal activities."

The pressure of his hands on her waist increased. Bending his head, he brushed his lips across hers.

"*All* activities?"

The pulse in Sam's neck fluttered wildly. "Yes." She breathed softly around her excitement-tightened throat. Taking a step nearer to him, she brought her hands up to cup his face, draw him closer. His hands held her body firmly away from his.

"Sam, stop," he groaned against her lips. "I'm filthy and sweaty."

Lightly her hands slid over his taut jaw, down his neck

185

to the front of his cotton work shirt. Her mouth still touching his, her fingers began opening the buttons.

"What are you doing?" Morgan murmured.

"Unbuttoning your shirt."

"I *know* that," he rasped. "But why?"

"I want you to swim with me."

"Sam," Morgan groaned hoarsely. "I've got to get cleaned up."

"The chlorine in the pool will clean you," Sam said complacently, tugging the shirt from his jeans. When the shirt was free, her hands went to his belt buckle, flipped it open. When the belt hung open, she opened the snap of his jeans and, caught at the zipper pull. One hand left her waist and covered her fingers, stilling their movement.

"Sara will see."

"No, she won't," Sam denied. "Both she and Jake are at home—playing grandparents." Her teeth nipped his lower lip. "We're alone till bedtime, Morgan."

She heard his sharply indrawn breath, then her hand was brushed aside. He stepped back, shrugging out of his shirt. He glanced up at her when his hands moved to complete the job she'd started on his zipper. Eyes dancing with deviltry, he teased, "Are you prepared to yank off my boots?"

"At your service, sir." Even in a bikini Sam's curtsy was graceful. "But I'd think it would be easier if you sat down."

Abandoning the jeans, Morgan dropped to the grass and lifted a very dirty booted foot. After much tugging and exaggerated grunting the boots were removed and his socks followed swiftly. Springing to his feet, Morgan released the pants zipper and stepped out of his jeans. His thumbs slid under the elastic of his very brief Jockey shorts, then he paused, black eyes skimming her bikini.

"The suit's got to go," he decided, laughing at her shocked face. "If I'm skinny dipping, so are you. Will you take it off," he grinned, "or will I?"

"Mor—gan," Sam pleaded.

"Either you take it off"—he took one step toward her—"or I will."

He dropped his briefs, kicked them aside, then waited, a small smile on his lips, while Sam removed the two skimpy pieces. As soon as they were gone, he held out his hand, grasped hers, and jumped into the pool.

"God that feels good," Morgan sighed when he surfaced. "How about you amusing yourself while I do a few laps, sluice the grime off my hide?"

"Be my guest," Sam waved a hand to encompass the pool. "Just don't be gone too long."

"I won't," he promised, shooting away from her.

Doing a slow sidestroke, Sam watched as Morgan's powerful arms cut cleanly through the water. After the fourth lap he came toward her. With hardly a break in motion his one arm caught her around the waist and he drew her with him to the side of the pool. Pinning her back to the smoothly painted wall, he growled, "I want my kiss."

"What kiss?" Sam asked, her eyes innocently wide.

"The kiss you've been teasing me with ever since I got home, you witch."

Planting himself firmly in front of her, he brought his mouth crashing onto hers. His lips were cool from the water and tasted slightly of chlorine. His tongue was hot and hungry. Excitement splintered through Sam's body sending tiny, sharp shards of pleasure along her veins. Her hands moved slowly up his chest, over his shoulders, loving the feel of his cool, wet skin.

"Let's get out of here."

Moving away from her, Morgan pushed himself up and over the edge of the pool, then turned to lift her out. She was no sooner on her feet than she was off again, swept up into Morgan's arms. Holding her tightly against his body, he strode to the house, his clothes and her bikini forgotten.

Once inside the bedroom, he kicked the door closed, dripped across the carpet, tossed her, soaking wet, onto the bed, and dropped down beside her, his mouth urgently seeking hers. Sam moaned a protest when his mouth left hers, then her face was caught, held still by his hard hands.

"Is it safe, Sam?" he grated harshly.

"Morgan, please," Sam whispered, her arms tightening around his neck, trying to bring his mouth back to her.

"Is it safe?" he demanded.

"Yes," Sam sighed, then, "Morgan?"

It was all the assurance, or plea, he needed. His hand moved, slowly, arousingly, from her face to her breasts, to her hips and back again to her breasts where they lingered, his fingers gentle, but exciting. His mouth demanded, his tongue searched, until she cried out with her need for him.

Their union, after so many weeks of abstinence, was wild and sweet and totally satisfying.

Her breathing returned to normal, and Sam lay in Morgan's arms, unmindful of the damp sheets. A soft sigh, almost a purr, escaped her lips at the delightful sensations Morgan's hand, stroking her thigh between hip and knee, created in her. Shifting his body, Morgan buried his face in the curve of her neck.

"You don't like taking those pills, do you?" he asked quietly.

"Morgan."

"Do you?" he insisted.

"No, I don't," Sam admitted reluctantly. "But it's all right, really, I—"

"Goddamnit, Sam," he grated roughly. "You should have let me have the vas—"

"No." Sam's tone was soft, but sharp with finality. "You'll change your mind some day, you'll see." She felt the movement of his forehead against her jaw as he shook his head.

"I need you, Sam," Morgan whispered close to her ear. "Not just for times like this, but all the time. I need to know you're mine, that you're here, that you're alive."

"Morgan, don't," Sam urged. "Don't talk about—"

"I must," he cut across her plea, "I must talk about it. Dear God, Sam," he groaned. "If it hadn't been for Babs and Ben, I'd have torn that hospital apart."

"Morgan, stop."

"I was so damned scared," he went on as if he hadn't heard her. "I felt that I had to get to you, help you, hold on to you to keep you from slipping away from me."

His arms jerked convulsively, crushing her to him so tightly Sam had to bite her lip to keep from crying out in pain. Her own arms held him fiercely, protectively, her hands smoothing over his tension-bunched muscles.

"I know, darling," she soothed softly when he shuddered. "I know."

I know now that this is some kind of man I married, she mused wonderingly. The gentle way he'd taken care of her through the long winter, into the spring, had amazed her. If Sara had fussed and clucked over her like a mother hen, Morgan had guarded her like a watchdog. In March, when she had cried and stormed at him that she was enormous and ugly, he had teased her out of her bad mood by declaring he liked the round, full look. And it had been such a bad winter. And he had worked such terribly long hours.

From their first meeting she'd thought he was unfeeling and hard. Over the winter she'd found out she'd been right on one count. He was hard. Hard and tough. The amount of hard, physical work he did appalled her. And as if that wasn't enough, he'd had to make several business trips. Each time he'd come home looking exhausted, and she'd found out, through Ben, by way of Babs, that he drove himself tirelessly in an effort to get home to her sooner.

The knowledge had induced feelings of guilt and she'd stared morosely at her steadily growing, increasingly clumsy body.

Who could have known? Even her doctor had not suspected. Had never, he admitted later, thought of ordering x rays.

When she'd gone into labor four weeks before her due date, Sam had panicked, Morgan had not. Talking to her quietly to calm her down, he'd made her comfortable in the Jag and driven at his usual high speed to the hospital. It was later, Sam learned from Babs, after they realized there were problems, that Morgan began pacing like a caged animal.

She had come very close, too close, to dying and although Sam was beyond the point of caring at the time, Babs later told her that they all knew and what the news did to Morgan was terrible to watch.

His eyes, Babs had said, were frightening and on several occasions he'd actually snarled in reply to what anyone said, even Ben. His long, rangy frame had measured the room countless times before the door had opened to admit Sam's doctor. And that poor man, Babs had laughed afterwards, had looked terrified when Morgan's head had

190

snapped around to him, his eyes narrowed dangerously, his teeth bared like a hungry dog's.

That, to Sam, was all hearsay. All she knew of those long hours was of crying out in agony for Morgan, and hanging on to life with all the will she possessed. When it was finally over, and she lay in a bed in a private room, her body spent, but her mind strangely alert, Morgan came to her.

The door opened and he stood there staring at her for long seconds. The same Morgan who was capable of endless hours of hard, physical work. The same Morgan who had promised to "drop" Jeff and would have. The same Morgan who had threatened to kill Duds and could have. That same Morgan stood staring at her, then walked to the bed, dropped to his knees beside it, lay his head on her breast, and wept. Wept with the release of bottled-up fear, as only a man, strong in himself, can weep.

"Have you seen them?" Sam's hands, looking white and fragile, smoothed his hair.

"No." His head moved from side to side in her hands.

"Go see," she urged softly. "They were worth it."

His head jerked up, his eyes luminous, but fiery, pinned hers.

"Nothing was worth it."

"They were."

Now Sam trembled in Morgan's crushing grip. Her convalescence had been so long, how good it felt to be with him like this again. Loosening his hold, Morgan lifted his head, his eyes, sharp with concern, studying her face.

"What's the matter? Are you cold?"

"No, I'm not cold." A becoming pink tinged her cheeks. "In fact just the opposite. Oh, Morgan, I want you to make love to me again before Sara brings the boys back."

"Our boys," Morgan chided softly, an enticing smile on his lips. "Our redheaded twins," he murmured. The smile twisted. "I love them so much, Sam. And they nearly killed you getting into the world."

"But they didn't," Sam whispered, the tip of her tongue teasing the corner of his mouth. "I'm alive, I'm here, and I'm yours."

Her words were stilled by the pressure of his mouth, her tongue was caught, entwined with his. When his tough, hard body moved against, then over, hers, she moaned in surrender. His mouth left hers to seek, tantalize, the gem-hard tip of her breast and she gasped, crying, "Yes, please, Morgan, make me your woman again."